She Thought She Was Immune.

It was him. His fault. He was huge, a man built to protect a woman from dragons, icy rains, danger. He was warm. And he was also demanding, because the pressure of his mouth never lessened until a foolish—totally inexcusable—whisper of longing escaped her throat.

He stepped back, but his knuckles brushed her cheek before he pulled his hand away. *"Cead mìle Fàilte,* Carra O'Neill. It's the Irish way of saying a hundred thousand welcomes."

She banished the dizziness, the heartbeat gone mad, the sudden swamping, restless ache.

"Mike?"

"Hmm?"

"We're going to work together just fine."

"I think so, too."

"Just so we know where we stand. You do that again and I'll knock your block off."

Dear Reader:

Welcome! You hold in your hand a Silhouette Desire—your ticket to a whole new world of reading pleasure.

A Silhouette Desire is a sensuous, contemporary romance about passions, problems and the ultimate power of love. It is about today's woman—intelligent, successful, giving—but it is also the story of a romance between two people who are strong enough to follow their own individual paths, yet strong enough to compromise, as well.

These books are written by, for and about every woman that you are—wife, mother, sister, lover, daughter, career woman. A Silhouette Desire heroine must face the same challenges, achieve the same successes, in her story as you do in your own life.

The Silhouette reader is not afraid to enjoy herself. She knows when to take things seriously and when to indulge in a fantasy world. With six books a month, Silhouette Desire strives to meet her many moods, but each book is always a compelling love story.

Make a commitment to romance—go wild with Silhouette Desire!

Best,

Isabel Swift
Senior Editor & Editorial Coordinator

JENNIFER GREENE
The Castle Keep

Silhouette Desire

Published by Silhouette Books New York

America's Publisher of Contemporary Romance

SILHOUETTE BOOKS
300 East 42nd St., New York, N.Y. 10017

Copyright © 1988 by Jennifer Greene

ISBN: 0-373-05439-4

First Silhouette Books printing August 1988

Printed in the U.S.A.

JENNIFER GREENE

lives on a centennial farm near Lake Michigan with her husband and two children. Before writing full-time, she worked as a personnel manager, counselor and teacher. Mid-1988 will mark the publication of her twenty-fifth romance. She claims the critical ingredient to success is a compassionate, kind, patient, understanding husband—who can cook.

Her writing has won national awards from Romance Writers of America, *Romantic Times* and *Affaire De Coeur*. She has also written under the pen name of Jeanne Grant.

One

The wind howled. The gods thundered. The skies shook. To add insult to injury, torrents of cold rain soaked Carra the moment she stepped out of the rental car. After traveling several thousand miles, her body was suffering fanciful delusions that it wanted an old robe, a mug of cocoa and a corner of a couch—any couch, but preferably a warm one with pillows.

To heck with the couch and the cocoa.

There it was.

Her "baby."

The Irish landscape was dramatic, lonely and wild, the stuff of mysticism and dreams. In the far distance slate-blue cliffs had a luminescent glow beneath a slash of lightning. The cliffs led down to rolling hills of gorse and grasses, flattened by the rage of the April storm. Closer in, fingers of rich, green land poked into the swollen Shannon, and the river waters flowed past in a blurring rush of silver.

All of it created an ideal setting for her "baby." Carra's gaze darted from turrets to towers, taking in the spell of Glencorrah Castle. The limestone structure was massive, impregnable and the color of gleaming washed pewter in the rain. A castle was built to withstand any siege; this one had withstood the siege of a dream too strong to die.

In the fourteenth century Master James of St. George had built the foundation for the most perfect castle of its kind. Glencorrah had been almost completed when he died. Six hundred years later his dream still stood. It wasn't totally restored or finished yet, but within weeks it would be.

The cold rain slushed through her hair. Carra firmly reminded herself that she could see the rest tomorrow. The castle wasn't going anywhere. She had bags to unpack, a cottage to find. Her stomach was grumbling, and it was going to be pitch black in another hour. No woman in her right mind would consider exploring on a night like this.

Carra tugged up the collar of her trench coat and sighed. She must have left her common sense in Boston, because her pumps were already skipping and dodging the mud puddles leading to the open drawbridge.

You've got one quick half hour, she told herself, but as soon as she reached the iron-studded doors of the barbican tower, she forgot about time. Finding her way was no problem. She would have known the layout blindfolded.

Once through the barbican, it was a simple matter of walking between the double curtain walls until she found a door to the main courtyard. The courtyard would lead her to the keep. She could wait for daylight to seriously explore the barbicans, towers and curtain walls, but how could she possibly come all this way without a look at Glencorrah's keep?

She found one door too choked with equipment and construction debris to allow passage. The second door opened easily, and the view darn near took her breath away. The courtyard contained a crazy blend of the fourteenth and twentieth centuries—an earth mover was stashed next to the smithy, cranes and bulldozers parked between the armory and stables—but those things hardly mattered.

In the heart of the yard was the keep, the main house in any castle. Glencorrah's stretched five stories tall, a fortress that would please any princess. A streak of lightning obligingly illuminated gothic arches and carved parapets, and the ribs of stone were a shout of courage and tenacity.

She loved it on sight, but crossing the mud bath of a yard was going to take another drenching. Mentally swearing at herself, she ducked her head and raced past the outer bailey, past the inner bailey and finally through the monstrously tall doors into the keep's foyer.

Once inside she shook herself like a puppy. She looked around and noticed that the foyer was all brooding shadows and gloom. The cold stone walls echoed every sound, every footstep, every breath. It was a fine place for a haunting, and it took a fair amount of scrambling over construction rubble before she reached the Great Hall.

The room stretched fifty feet tall, with ceiling beams larger around than she was. Her imagination filled up the huge, yawning space in no time.

Minstrels belonged on the upper decks. Ladies in wimples and gold girdles should be sewing in the arched windows. Piles of furniture would be inappropriate in the Great Hall, but there should be trestle tables mounded with food—a roasted boar, vegetables, pewter steins of ale. Knights in full armor would pay homage to their lord here; the steward would be giving daily orders to a dozen pages.

If Carra did her job, the minstrels and knights, the roasted boar and tapestries, were all going to be real two months from now. The Irish government—through a gentleman named James Killimer—had hired her, very literally, to make Glencorrah come alive.

If she could do it.

A few years ago when the Glencorrah project was first conceived, Carra had never doubted her ability to do the job. The Irish had wanted an American medieval historian, because it was American tourist dollars they wanted to draw. The concept of making a castle into a living museum was brand-new. They'd needed imagination more than specific skills, initiative more than experience. Carra had thought then, and still did, that her passionate belief in Glencorrah had gotten her the job.

She still believed in the castle project. It was herself she'd lost faith in. At twenty-four she'd had more sass and confidence than sense. She was twenty-seven now and knew exactly how hard real courage was to find.

A woman could make shattering mistakes in three years. Unforgivable mistakes. The kind of mistakes that made a woman doubt who she was, what she was worth, what she was capable of.

Carra looked around the room in awe. Her doubts and anxieties didn't suddenly disappear but they did diminish. The castle's enchantment made one woman's problems seem small. History had always woven a powerful spell around her, but never more than now.

Someone else might see nothing but damp, cold stone; she saw the promise of something lasting and strong. A different woman might crinkle her nose at the construction dust or shiver at the haunted, dark emptiness. Carra saw something to hold on to.

She needed something to hold on to. Desperately.

Normally Micheal Dougel Fitzgerald relished noise, clutter and people in vast quantities. Still, a man had an occasional need for time alone. Mike had work to do, and at the first sound of a clipped footstep below, his concentration was broken.

He waited, though he was loathe to strip the hide off the trespassers if he could help it. The local kids made a regular habit of ignoring Glencorrah's No Trespassing signs. The deserted castle made for an irresistible meeting place for lovers. He'd told the kids at least a dozen times that between the equipment and machinery and construction messes, the place wasn't safe. Still, he didn't like the idea of yelling at the townspeople.

The footsteps kept coming. When he finally realized that they weren't going to stop and they weren't going away, he tossed down his pencil and strode toward the inside window ledge. His shaggy brows knitted into a thundercloud scowl. The kids had already figured out that his bark was worse than his bite, but they had to be intimidated by a full-blown Fitzgerald rage. He'd worked himself into a good fake blustery mood when he saw her.

From three stories down he could see the woman was shivering cold and wetter than a drowned rat. For his first glimpse her back was toward him. Her shoulders were hunched inside a dripping raincoat, her hands splayed at her sides, her face tilted toward the faint light in the south window.

She didn't seem to know she was cold, didn't seem to notice the rain. The way she stood made him think of passion. Pride. Hope. And then she turned.

Her face was ivory pale and her hair a rich, dark sable. The coat hid her figure, and the shadowed gloom denied him a clear look at her features. He could make out that her cheekbones had an elegant slant, that her mouth was red and small and soft looking. She had dark brows with a fragile arch, and she walked like old money, regal and quiet. She was of average height, and he guessed slight in build.

He meant to announce himself and let on he was there and somehow didn't. She obviously believed herself alone.

He watched her roam, absorbed in the mortar and stone, trailing her fingers along walls and archways. Thunder growled; rain raged down in a splashing hiss.

She didn't seem to notice. She touched stone as if it were fragile, as if she could make it warm under her fingertips. As if it were a lover she could bring to life.

The romantic stirred him always. Why else was he drawn here night after night? Especially at night, when the weathered castle walls whispered of six hundred years of lonely emptiness. The wind blew cold through the castle windows, made a keening sound that echoed in all the dark corners. Micheal would have admitted to loneliness to no man. No one who knew him would even have guessed.

The woman below, though, was lonely in a way he understood all too well. There was a level of loneliness that was painful, naked, raw.

And she was damned beautiful. The minutes ticked past. Her sable mat was drying, starting to swirl softly around her cheeks. She seemed to wear her hair smooth and simple and in an even length with a shag of bangs. He couldn't make out the color of her eyes, but they were light. If the color eluded him, he saw the haunting sadness in her eyes every time she faced in his direction.

Three hundred crushing tons of rock and mortar wasn't doing much of a job at comforting her. She needed a lover. Now.

About the same instant that thought occurred to him, he dragged a hand through his hair with a rueful expression. How crazy could you get? He was thirty-four. Too old to play amateur psychologist with a stranger, too honest to spy on another human being's private moments and too practical to watch a woman work herself into a case of pneumonia without doing something about it.

"Hey, down there!"

"Pardon?" She pivoted around, fast. "Who's there? Where are you?"

"I'm up here." It took him a moment before he could say anything else. Her voice was low for a woman. Low, throaty and distinctive. Until that moment it had never crossed his mind that she wasn't Irish. "American? And you've come a long way to trespass if that was the twang of the East Coast I heard."

"I'm not trespassing!" Carra finally spotted the man on the inside window ledge, but all she could really see was a shaggy head of bright hair and a brawny bulk of dark shoulders in a black sweatshirt. Nothing she saw made her pulse stop pumping adrenaline. The shadowed giant seemed to come out of nowhere. "Are you part of the Glencorrah project?"

Another pause. "Oh, God. The accent's Boston."

"Yes," she agreed impatiently. He sounded either amused or rueful. Carra was neither. "Look—"

"I am. Darnit, that's half the problem." In the shadowed alcove she saw him drag a hand through his hair. "I've always been fond of a good coincidence, but the blend of Boston and Glencorrah is too tough even for me to buy. You have to be my resident medieval historian? Not only arrived seven days early, but definitely packaged differently than expected. There's a reasonably usable stone staircase beyond the west arch. Come on up, Carra O'Neill."

"Wait a minute." She stood stock-still. "Who are you?"

"The man sharing architectural credits for this monster with a long dead gent by the name of Master James of St. George. Ring a bell?"

A zillion of them. "You're not Micheal Fitzgerald," she announced.

He believed that was called a withering tone. It wasn't hard to recognize. Every time he was in trouble as a kid, his mother had pronounced his full name with that same lethal inflection. He'd been in a lot of trouble as a kid.

Possibly he was in trouble now. The woman below not only bore no relationship to his mother, but none to the preconceived image he had of Carra O'Neill. The woman below looked like a lover. A slightly drowned, slightly irritated lover. And his pulse, nerves, hormones and imagination all recognized a woman he wanted—intended—to know.

Assuming he managed to raise her first impression of him a little higher than root canals, taxes, wet puddles. "The name is Mike." He tried to make his tone disarmingly friendly. "You might as well climb up here before you catch your death—I've got a blanket and some food. When did your flight get in, and why on earth didn't you call and let me know you were coming this much ahead of schedule?"

"I . . ." She swallowed whatever she started to say and started again. "I'll be right there." She strode toward the far arched doors and disappeared from his sight.

He heard her clipped heels on the staircase as he climbed off the ledge. Somewhere in the mess on the long table was a wicker basket with the remnants of his dinner. He pushed aside the thermos of coffee and searched for the flask.

Glencorrah's solar was technically the lord and lady's bedchamber, but for the past two months Mike had used it as an office, first-aid station and private refuge. Amenities were few. The arched Norman windows let in nothing but a cold, fast-falling night and the shuddering gloom of a thunderstorm. Blueprints were scattered on the long table; hard hats stacked beneath it. The cot was a natural stash for spare tools.

And at a glance, he could see that she wasn't impressed. The room caught her attention well enough, but he didn't rate a second look. He could finally see that she had blue eyes. They weren't a hard blue like a sapphire, but a luminous, clear blue like the sky at sunrise. Her eyes were capable of a certain chill. In fact, he figured they were capable of freezing most men at three paces.

Possibly she took offense at the flask of Ireland's best. Either that or she had a definite aversion to six-foot-three-inch men with red hair and bull chests.

He reminded himself that she couldn't know he'd been staring at her all that time as he pressed a brimming shot glass into her hand. "It'll warm you up; then we'll get you something to eat. And if you'll strip off that wet coat, I've got either a blanket or you can use my dry jacket...." He glanced around, then tried his most winsome grin. "The jacket's somewhere. I seem to have an annoying habit of losing anything that isn't tied down—there it is. You look half frozen."

"I'm fine. Mr. Fitzgerald—"

"Mike."

"Mike then." Carra switched the shot glass to her left hand and offered him her right. "I'm honored to meet you."

His hand swallowed hers. He felt the softness of her skin, the slight dampness that indicated nerves and a distinctly feminine firmness and a *we will be businesslike* attitude. That was unfortunate. Although laid-back came with the family genes, Mike had never mastered businesslike.

She said something about not wanting to interrupt him, never expecting to meet anyone tonight, knowing what she looked like after tramping through the rain. He didn't really listen. Polite talk never interested him; her eyes did.

She had a closed-in demeanor—sensuality banked in a proper posture, emotion schooled into a fancy smile—but the vulnerability in her soft blue eyes was real. Her vulnerability touched him. "Don't mind me. I'm bound to quit staring at you any minute now," he said humorously. "I guess I'm still looking for the tweeds and bulging briefcase."

"You had a few preconceptions of what a medieval historian would look like?"

"Sure. Lots." He motioned to her coat, crooking his finger impatiently. When she finally shrugged out of it, he understood her hesitation. Her silk blouse with the froth of lace was a long way from tweeds. The blouse and the swish of jewel-tone skirt announced she had hopelessly feminine taste in clothes and a lithe slim figure designed to catch a man's imagination. "You formed preconceptions, too, didn't you? Two bits says you were expecting Mr. Yuppie in a blue-striped shirt and an alligator tie."

He found his jacket, draped it over her shoulders and resisted the urge to let his hands linger. She was wary enough. Also hungry, he figured. He foraged through the basket and came up with bread, a wedge of cheese and an apple.

"I never thought about what you would look like one way or another," Carra denied. A giant lie.

"No? You're getting a little color back in your face. Another four or five hours and you just might dry out. Sit down, for heaven's sake."

Balancing the wedge of cheese, bread and the glass, she eased down to a corner of a cot. There wasn't any other place to sit. She took a quick sip from the shot glass and grimaced. The amber liquid had a sting, and it slid down her throat like fire.

She didn't want the whiskey, she didn't want the cheese, and she'd definitely changed her mind about coming to Ireland. Micheal Fitzgerald was a huge, strapping giant man with a thatch of copper hair, green eyes and a jaw covered with the stubble of an evening beard. He wore his jeans tight, his sweatshirt loose and had an incorrigibly cocky grin.

His appearance couldn't have been of less importance to her, except that it was so different from what she'd anticipated. The one doubt she'd never had about this trip was that she'd enjoy working with this man. Labels like *brilliant* and *creative* were often tagged after the Fitzgerald name, and his background was intensive in both architecture and geology. Before meeting him she'd enthusiastically pegged him as an achiever, an ambitious man with outstanding skills and the drive and dedication to carry him through.

Maybe he was just that. She simply needed a moment to reconcile the image of the man she'd anticipated calling a respectful "sir" with this throwback Pict-Irish of the sexy eyes.

Her own ancestry was just as Irish as his. Three generations of American citizenship hadn't diluted her obvious heritage. Her own coloring, though, came from the oldest settlers in Ireland, the Iberian Celts named "Fir Bolg." They were a small, dark-haired people, who were happy with the island kingdom of Erin they'd settled nearly two thousand years ago.

That old history wouldn't have come to mind now but for Mike. The Celts had been perfectly content until a second race of people had streamed through Ireland. The Picts were a tall, fair-skinned people with tawny red hair and green eyes. They called themselves the Tribes of the Goddess Dana and were mystically inclined. All the Irish tales of druids and fairies came from the Picts. Historically—and there was no question of this as far as Carra was concerned—all the trouble the Irish had ever known had also come from the Picts.

Mike's genes were unmistakable.

He had a right to professional curiosity, of course. But there was a giant difference between evaluating the potential of a co-worker and staring at a woman as if she were an lamb chop.

"Believe me, I won't take up much more of your time," she assured him blandly. "You were obviously working, and I just got here, haven't unpacked yet, haven't even found my lodgings—"

"Haven't finished your cheese yet, either." Faster than he could refill her shot glass, she had her hand over the top. "Rather have coffee?"

"Much rather," she admitted.

There wasn't much left in his thermos, but he managed half a mug. "Whether coffee or whiskey, we need a toast. To the land of the little people and your stay in Erin."

"That's not necess—"

"Sure it is." Mike wasn't sure why, but relaxing her was necessary, so was feeding her and making sure she was warm. She wasn't exactly stiff, but her groping for a casually friendly attitude didn't cover up her feelings of awkwardness. He felt like telling her that no woman felt awkward around Micheal Dougel Fitzgerald, but he was too busy feeling slammed in his midsection.

At thirty-four he'd certainly felt that slam with a woman before. Just not quite this way. The sexual zing was sweet and strong. The lace and haunted, soft eyes and long, slim hands were sugar. The gravely low voice and pride and classy, cool smile were spice.

A thought dawdled through his mind. *We'll have to find out who hurt you, Irish. And then we'll see.* The wayward thought was banished, as it should be. God knew where it had even come from. God also knew she was sending him every steady *no* signal in a woman's invisible, considerable repertoire.

So he talked work until her voice dropped that stilted catch. Inconsequential comparisons of their home bases—San Francisco versus Boston—cut more ice. By the time he put her empty mug back in his basket, her shoulders had lost their duchess rigidity, and he moved on to the subject of Glencorrah.

"You bring some special qualifications to this project," he told her honestly. "Killimer sent me a list of the people who'd applied for the medieval historian's job."

"All of whom had a ton more years' experience than I did?" she guessed wryly.

"Some did," he agreed. "But no one else had spent their spare time in places like Williamsburg and Connor's Prairie. You not only had a background in successful American 'living museums', but you put on paper the hows and whats and whys of making those concepts work for Glencorrah. No one else took that kind of initiative, showed that kind of enthusiasm. You loved this place long before you laid eyes on it, didn't you?"

"Yes." She couldn't deny it, didn't even try.

"Me, too. Although I expect for very different reasons. I still have some suspicions the Irish only hired me by default. Couldn't find another architect crazy enough to want to work with several thousand tons of brick and mortar on a shifting sand and clay floodplain. Master James of St. George sure picked a helluva site six hundred years ago."

"Is our baby stable?" Carra demanded swiftly.

He chuckled at her expression as he dragged his work stool closer to the cot, dropped down on it and hooked his feet on the rungs. "She's stable. Now."

"I take it you've had your share of troubles."

"Months of them, but then that's why I took the job. It's like when you're four—a stolen sucker always tastes better than the one your mom's approved of. Easy's no fun. Challenges keep the blood moving . . . and that subject's not what we started with. I was trying to tell you, short and sweet, that I'm glad you're here."

"Thanks." He seemed to mean it. The last half hour had submarined her initial wariness. Who would have guessed he would be so disarmingly easy to talk to? And exhaustion was starting to hit her in waves. For two cents she'd lean her head back, curl her legs under her and go to sleep. "We both know you're really the one with the terrific qualifications. I'm hoping we'll work well together."

"We'll work well together. We'll also practically be roommates for the next two months."

"Pardon?" Her eyes whipped up. "I understood the Irish were putting us up in separate cottages."

"They did, but the cottages are as close as a spit and a promise. Isolated from the regular work crew, which is just as well."

"Problems?"

His eyes settled with disturbing intensity on her face. "Probably nothing you weren't already expecting. The boys are a rowdy group, and you must have realized before this that you're the lone woman. Better than a hundred men have been pinned on this construction site for the last two months, if you get my drift. On top of that, there just might be a wee prejudice built up against a woman with authority, one who's an American at that.''

She anchored a strand of hair behind her ear; her pulse picked up a worried beat. ''How bad is this 'wee prejudice'?'' She watched him take out a pocket knife to peel an apple.

When the task was done he handed it to her. Again she felt his deliberate assessment of her face. ''Nothing you'll have to handle alone. We make a natural alliance, being the only two Americans involved in the project.''

Her teeth sliced into the sweet-tart fruit. He was leaving something out. It took her a minute before she figured out what it was. ''If by any chance you were harboring a worry that I took this job because of the man to woman ratio. . . .''

He had the brightest green eyes she'd ever seen on a man. ''I never said that.''

''No? But it's just occurring to me what a mucky business Mr. Killimer threw you when he hired me. A male historian would have been easier, wouldn't it? For all you knew, I could have been a latent nympho or a feminist dragging around miles of emotional baggage.'' Her tone was deliberately light, but her tongue still tasted the tang of the apple. Forbidden fruit? The subject was touchy, but darnit, it had to be. ''Rest easy, Mike. That off-balance man to woman ratio didn't draw me; it darn near kept me from taking the job. Talk's cheap, I know, but you'll see soon enough that I have no interest in bothering your men—or encouraging anyone's interest in me. It won't happen. Believe it.''

She was quick and perceptive, Mike thought, in the sense that she'd picked up his professional need to know what her attitude toward the men was going to be. Truthfully he'd already guessed her stance, just like he already knew he was going to have his hands full once the crew got a look at her.

That was his problem, not hers. Hers interested him far more.

She didn't have to announce to the world in bright red letters that she was off men. Her Boston-bred cool did a terrible job of eclipsing the vulnerable woman he'd first spotted below. Her warmth was natural. Humor and honesty bubbled to the surface the longer they talked. The cool formality was simply her first-line defense. All it took to spear the crust was his taking a "pals" attitude.

Ah, sweetheart, he thought. Pals will only work so far. The electricity's so strong in this room I can taste it. Can't you feel it, just a little?

He steered the conversation away from work. Outside the dark storm still raged. He told her about his five brothers and sisters, his family, how he'd gained a reputation as a renegade in the architectural field. The foolish woman not only listened, but laughed in all the right spots. It was her own darn fault he took so long to get the conversation back to her.

"Didn't it get to you on the drive from the Shannon airport?"

"Get to me?" she echoed curiously.

His grin was full of dance. "Ireland. I'd underestimated her draw. The mists off the river; the greens and the hillsides haunted with ghosts of Connemara and Derryveagh. The people around here still believe in luck and mysticism and the little people; some say it's catching.''

She said dryly, "So's chicken pox. Luckily I'm immune.''

His green eyes lingered on hers for a moment, curiously intense, almost piercing. And then he threw back his head. His laugh was a boom, delightful and open. "I take it the romance of the Irish doesn't move you, Carra O'Neill?''

She shook her head. "What romance? Ireland's tourist image never cut much mustard with me. Black and Decker is the largest employer in Kildare, and there's a Nippon plant in Ballivor. From Waterford crystal to the oil being harvested in the North Sea, I never thought the Irish were so whimsical or impractical when it counted.''

"Maybe they're not, but maybe I guessed that you were.''

"Me?''

"You locked on medieval history as a career, not everyone's choice. Surely it was the romance that first caught your interest? You know what I mean. Knights in armor and jousts and the impossible dream. Ladies with those long veils and Arthur's sword and the code of chivalry...''

"You're not serious.''

"Sure I am.''

She chuckled. "Ah, Mike, you need a real history lesson. There was nothing romantic about medieval times. Chivalry was strictly a code of war that had nothing to do with protecting women. And life in a real castle wasn't fun—but it sure was short. Idealizing that time is impossible. The reality was living with drafts and disease and a deplorable lack of sanitation."

His mouth twitched. "So much for romantic stereotypes?"

"Put 'em to bed," she advised. "None of them will hold more water than a sieve."

"You're destroying some of my favorite illusions," he protested with a gravity that had her chuckling again.

"I doubt that! Anyway, that's really my job, to make Glencorrah a medium where people can see what medieval life was honestly like. There were no knights in shining armor. Not then. Not now. Not ever."

"You sound damn sure of that, Carra O'Neill."

A quick retort was on the tip of her tongue, but somehow it never got said. Mike's voice had suddenly turned low, intimately quiet. She found her smile suddenly hovered in a limbo of uncertainty. His eyes were focused on her face with a look so bold and direct that she felt a shimmer of lush, powerful awareness.

The feeling shook her to her toes. She hadn't traveled several thousand miles to be disarmed by a big, bold man with charm and a cheeky grin. She studied him, hard.

His shaggy eyebrows were the color of fire; his chin had a small scar. His skin had a sunbaked color that brought out the brilliant green of his eyes, and he had strong, square features. Character lines framed his eyes and mouth. He'd definitely been around the block a few times. He'd known women. And he took in life like he took in air, easy and natural, with an implicit male sensuality that undoubtedly had most women honing their fanciest seduction skills.

Not her.

If there was one man she needed to get along with at Glencorrah, it was Micheal Fitzgerald. Beyond friendliness and camaraderie, though, there was a closed door, a locked cell, a violent *no*—in her head and in her heart.

Carra had learned a long time ago that there were no knights for her. She'd learned that lesson hard, and she'd learned it painfully. Of course, she'd recognized the little hum of attraction between them the moment she walked into the solar. Hums could be ignored. She'd done it before.

Mike saw the play of emotions on her face. She'd been open, warm, smiling. No more. It was like watching a door slam. The mat of soft, black lashes shielded her eyes; pride ruled her shoulders, and the barest hint of defiance set the line of her lips.

Fascinating. Slowly, most reluctantly, he shifted to his feet. "Enough talking. I keep forgetting how tired you have to be. If I can hitch a ride, I'll get you settled at the cottage."

"I don't need settling in, but if you need a ride, you've got one." She hurried to stand up when he did. Her voice was courteous, but its tone could have frozen the Amazon River.

He folded the blanket, grabbed his basket. "Good. The cottages are within walking distance, except in a downpour. I wasn't relishing the thought of the walk tonight."

"I hope it doesn't rain like this every day?" She quickly took off his jacket and glanced around for her coat.

"Just keep the jacket. You can't put on that wet coat again. And as far as the rain, the cloudbursts are pretty regular. They say a true Irishman can identify forty shades of green. They neglect to mention all the water it takes to get those damn greens."

She laughed, but it wasn't a real laugh. The change in her mood made him think of dynamite volatility. On the way down the staircase he naturally put a guiding hand at the small of her back—the stairway was dark, shadowed, steep. He'd meant nothing by the contact. She tensed as if his palm were a knife.

It gave him pause. It would seem he'd inherited two Carra O'Neills in his medieval historian. One was a realist with a quick mind and a snap to her humor. The other was the lady who forgot pouring rain to explore a musty, dank castle alone, passion in her eyes, softness and fragility radiating from her.

Both women interested him, but it was the former who rated casual contact up there with bullets, whose blue eyes dared a man to be attracted to her.

Two

By the time they reached Carra's rental car, the rain had lessened to a mere maddening drizzle, and the sky was a rolling dark black.

"I could drive," Mike offered.

Carra shook her head. "I'll be glad to. But if you'd give me directions?"

"Just follow the road to the left around the castle. You'll reach the turnoff in less than a quarter of a mile."

For Mike it was a long quarter of a mile. She popped the clutch, stalled the car and finally revved into reverse. He figured out pretty quick that she'd rarely handled a stick shift, wasn't too fond of left-handed driving and went entirely too fast. Who would have guessed that this quiet medieval historian from Boston College had a secret wish to race at Le Mans?

"Carra?"

"Hmm?"

"Don't you think it's a little dark to drive without lights?" he asked mildly.

Color skated up her throat as she found the lights knob. Even though she kept her eyes on the road, Mike was distracting her.

The giant took up half the front-seat space with his knees alone. He leaned against the door and had one hand on his knee and his left arm thrown over the seat back. His fingers were inches from her shoulders. The tops of his hands had a light dusting of sand-colored hair. They were big hands, ringless, strong, callused. He sat loose-limbed and easy and in a way that made his jeans provocatively hug his thighs. His boots were made of good leather.

Considering that it was pitch black and she wasn't interested, she'd noticed an awful lot. Lips in a firm line, Carra kept the pedal to the metal. Driving soothed her; it always had. Except now. She felt as jumpy as a kite in a gale. Mike had done nothing to justify the adrenaline pumping through her bloodstream. It all came from her.

His ringless hands were none of her business. The fit of his jeans was none of her business. Mike was an incorrigibly overwhelming man. So?

So her pulse was humming and her nerves were on edge. He'd been friendly, warm, easy to talk to. She couldn't have prayed for the basics of a better working relationship with Glencorrah's chief architect. He may have looked at her with more than professional interest, but she could handle that. *No* was the easiest word to use in the English vocabulary.

You're simply overtired, Carra, she told herself. And she knew that was true. Like a faulty computer program, her emotions were simply responding to inappropriate stimuli. Once she had some sleep everything would be fine. Establishing distance from Micheal Fitzgerald was an even quicker priority. She found the turnoff and seconds later braked to a spine-jarring stop.

"That was quite a ride," Mike said lazily. "Ever think about the Indy 500 tryouts?"

She blinked, then offered him a wry look. "You're here safe and sound, aren't you?"

"Not all of me. Could we go back and pick up my nerves at the castle?"

She chuckled, but as she climbed out of the car, she forgot all about Mike, and the past thirty frazzled traveling hours. The dip in the road had led to a pocket of charm.

The drizzly dark night would have made it impossible to see if it weren't for a pair of wrought-iron yard lights. Two thatched-roof cottages sat side by side, each with latch-hooked doors and rough stone walls. Wild roses climbed their sides, illuminated in the lights' halo, their scent sweetened by the night and rain. She couldn't see the Shannon River, but she could smell it. The whisper of sea air and mist both soothed and wooed her senses.

Mike couldn't take his eyes off her face. During the drive she'd exercised all the off-limits body language that a woman could use. In fact, she could purse her lips tighter than any schoolmarm he'd ever met...but her lips weren't pursed now. Her eyes had a yearning softness, her mouth a raw vulnerability.

It seemed only buildings brought out the lover in Carra. He wondered dryly how comforting she found rock and stone in the middle of the night. "You like the cottages?"

"*Love* them," she said softly. "I didn't know what the accommodations would be, and I didn't care. For two months I could have camped out anywhere for the chance to work on Glencorrah. But this..."

The trunk slammed behind her. Mike had her two suitcases in his hands. Both, she knew, weighed as if they were filled with bricks. She rushed toward him. "I'll get one—"

"I can handle them—but we have temporary problems of another kind, I'm afraid. You're here an unexpected week early. I haven't checked your place out or had it stocked with food."

"It's okay," she said lightly. "Believe me, I've coped with lots worse than this. I'll be fine." Silvery rain shimmered in her hair; she didn't notice. All she could see was the cottage.

He pushed open the door, deposited her suitcases inside and straightened. He believed that she had, at some time and some way, coped with lots worse than this.

By lamplight her features were impossibly fragile. Exhaustion gave her skin a mesmerizing translucence. And the proud tilt of her shoulders suggested that she expected to handle all the real and imaginary crises in life alone. He said slowly, "Don't get bogged down on pretty, Irish. If you haven't worked with a peat fire before—''

''I won't have any problems, honestly. Whatever I run into I can handle.''

He hesitated. It didn't take a mind reader to figure out that she wanted him gone. She was exhausted, he knew. She was also excellent at building high, tall walls. Her smile was blank and impersonal. Her cheery expression was as impenetrable as granite.

It took him a moment to realize the capital crime he'd committed. He'd looked at her the way a man looks at a woman who interests him. If she'd been bothered less, she'd be thinking instead of reacting. He tried again. ''Look, you may just be walking into more of a camping-out situation than you bargained for. It wouldn't take me any time at all to help you get settled in.''

''Thanks, but it's really not necessary.'' Again she smiled, this time brilliantly. Her palms were damp, and blood inexcusably zipped up and down her veins.

She'd had enough of all this nonsense. She wanted to be alone inside the thatched-roof haven. For reasons she had no intention of examining, Mr. Fitzgerald was raising her blood pressure. Solitude would cure that ailment just fine.

But she wasn't alone yet. The gleam of his copper hair had turned mahogany in the rain. His shoulders came close to filling the doorway. The darkness magnified the power of his size and the physical strength implicit in long, muscled legs and bear chest. For the first time she noticed that his smile was missing.

Was he waiting for something? It occurred to her that she was, too. Lightly, warmly, she experimented with a maternal tone. "You've been a brick, filling me in on everything, Mike. I really appreciate it." She motioned vaguely toward the cottages. "It's pretty obvious we're going to be living on top of each other. I want you to know I won't take advantage of that. On the job or off, I expect to find my own way, take care of myself."

He fed her the next line, slow and easy. "And you especially don't want any special privileges because you're the lone woman in the group?"

"Exactly. I don't want you worrying that you're stuck with the clinging vine type for a co-worker."

"Somehow that thought never crossed my mind."

"Good."

The small word seemed to pop the lid on his patience. She sounded so very sure that she'd just plastered a solid layer of mortar in a very thick wall. Mike had made a career out of building walls, but he figured if he didn't do something pretty quick to tear this one down, Carra's defenses were going to rival that cement fence in China. "I think you do an excellent job of letting a man know exactly where he stands, Carra—but we still can't have you traveling halfway across the world without a decent welcome."

"Pardon?"

She'd been waiting for him to move, yet he couldn't have shocked her more when he did. His fingers propped up her chin, and within the space of a bare second his mouth covered hers.

The kiss started as a sassy peck. If it had just stayed that way she wouldn't have had any problems. Instead, that first skimming pressure sent a rolling shock wave of surprise through him. Through her. The speed of light was fast, but not half as fast as the speed of darkness.

He murmured something low; his arms stole around her, and his lips suddenly turned wooing, sting-soft, coaxing. Her oxygen stopped flowing somewhere between her throat and her lungs. She tasted whiskey and apples and the flavor of raw, male impatience.

Shock meshed with a sudden unbearable weakness. Shattering weakness. Instincts had already warned her that Micheal making a pass was possible, but not now. Not like this. She'd never expected that Mike was a man who knew how to kiss, who liked to kiss, who had a very definite idea of what a woman's lips were made for.

She meant to bolt. But it was so dark. The steel texture of his thighs anchored against her, and the chill rain contrasted to the warmth of his mouth, his tongue. She felt crushed between the scents of leather and whiskey, disarmed by his dominant size and the tenderness in his rough callused hands. She could tell that he liked her mouth, and his tongue offered her a heady, appreciative, dangerously intimate dissertation on exactly how much he loved the taste of her.

So much time had passed since she'd felt yearning for a man's touch. She'd thought she was immune. It was him. His fault. He was huge, a man built to protect a woman from dragons, icy rains, danger. He was warm. She'd found life a ceaseless cold war. And he was also demanding. She knew because the pressure of his mouth never lessened until a rash, totally inexcusable whisper of longing escaped her throat.

He lifted his head slowly, a dark frown embedded in his forehead as he studied her face. A swift kiss was all he'd originally intended. A chance to show her that a man was a lot warmer than rock and stone. A need to wipe off the formal, distant smiles and find out if the lover—the crushable warm-blooded lover of a woman he'd first seen at the castle—was real.

He found out what he wanted to know, but he hadn't expected his world to get shaken in the process. Her response had been so wild and fragile that it took his breath away. He thought of wet roses and fire. He saw the silk mist of desire in her eyes and a naked vulnerability he had no business tampering with.

And for the second time since he'd met her, he thought that Carra O'Neill was a a woman who needed a knight. A man to whisk her away on a fast, white steed and protect her, keep her, love her until the haunted sadness disappeared from her eyes and she gave that passionate response willingly and freely.

Mike, at thirty-four, was no woman's knight. He was just a man, and obviously the blundering variety. He'd never meant to lay bare fragile feelings, never meant to hurt her.

Give her space, Fitzgerald, he thought. And for God's sake play this light and natural. He stepped back, but his knuckles almost involuntarily brushed her cheek before he took his hand away. "*Céad míle fáilte,* Carra O'Neill. It's the Irish way of saying a hundred-thousand welcomes."

She banished the dizziness, the heartbeat gone mad, the sudden swamping, restless ache. Only because she was a born and bred lady, who happened to abhor all violence, did she resist the urge to swing a fist at his languid, lazy grin. "Mike?"

He was already halfway out the door. "Hmm?"

"We're going to work together just fine," she told him.

"I think so, too."

"Just so we know where we stand. You do that again and I'll knock your block off."

She heard his roar of a laugh—dammit, the man even laughed with full powered emotion—and then he was gone. She could hear his cottage door click open and closed, and she was left alone in the rain and darkness.

Two hours later she stretched and rolled her knuckles at the small of her back. No amount of exhaustion had been able to subdue the feminine instinct to settle in. Her frenzy of energy was linked to a man's kiss she couldn't get out of her mind, but worrying about that problem was again postponed.

She took a moment to simply enjoy what would be her refuge for the next two months. The cottage was dollhouse size, just two rooms and a bath. The walls were white-washed stone, and the ceilings were slanted. A floor-to-ceiling fireplace dominated the main room. When she'd first walked in, the table and two-seater couch and chair had been lined up against the wall like soldiers.

She'd regrouped them, turned on lights, set out books, fluffed pillows, made the room hers. There was nothing she could rearrange in the bedroom, but also nothing she had to. The bedroom was tiny, but the old-fashioned rope bed was covered with a marvelous handmade quilt and delicate Irish lace curtains framed the windows.

The bathroom was so old it had a ceiling pull for the john, a white porcelain tub with claw feet and no shower. She didn't care. She also didn't care that the electric lights wavered like dizzy drunks and that the water pressure was marginal. It took her forever to realize that the brick-sized blocks by the fireplace were peat—fire fuel—and her first attempt to start a fire caused more smoke than warmth because the damper stuck. She didn't care about that, either.

The cottage already had her scent, her belongings, her stamp in all the corners. Inconveniences had never bothered her; she loved the history and the character and the feeling of coziness. Dark, cold rain continued to pelt on the windows outside. She was in. Safe, secure, warm and alone.

Finally there was nothing left to fuss with. She found a nightgown, her hairbrush and toothpaste. When she washed her face, her eyes met their match in the cracked bedroom mirror. Never mind how tired she was, she looked different. Stronger. More confident. Maybe it was just being here. She was miles from home, miles from everything familiar. And for hours now, she hadn't once thought about the loss of the baby.

Her eyes squeezed closed; she forced them open again. She rinsed her mouth, brushed her hair and started peeling off clothes.

In principle a woman should easily recover from a pregnancy that had never gone beyond the third month. Carra had miscarried long before she'd ever felt the baby quicken. Family and friends had never realized she was carrying a child—and still didn't know. The doctor had warned her that a slight depression was common after a miscarriage.

She hadn't suffered a slight depression. Her entire world had shattered. She'd read enough on the subject to know that a miscarriage was often an act of God for a baby not strong or not right or who was never equipped to survive. That wasn't true of her baby.

Her baby would have survived... if Carra had had better judgment. The guilt was on her plate, and the plate refused to wash clean.

She'd closed up in a rage of guilt and an iceberg of numbness. On the surface she'd gone on with her studies and her classes and her life. Freshman students packed her classes. Boston College afforded her special privileges for the extra responsibilities she took on. Family and friends filled her free time. None of it made any difference.

She hadn't felt a damn thing in two years.

In the bedroom she pushed back the quilt and shivered as she slid into the icy-cold sheets. The mattress was soft and thick—feathers, she guessed—and a little lumpy. She tucked up a knee and curled until she found a comfortable spot.

As fast as she closed her eyes, she envisioned Mike. She released a loud, impatient sigh in the darkness. She knew exactly why his kiss had gotten to her, why the man had disturbed her from the moment she met him.

He'd had the annoying, irritating, upsetting nerve to make her feel.

She didn't want to feel—anything—although she'd ironically come to Glencorrah to force herself back into life. Guilt wasn't bringing the baby back, and neither was living in limbo. She'd had courage once. Surely some forgiving could take place if she never made another mistake, never once failed in judgment again, never, *never* let her heart rule her head.

As a castle symbolized self-sufficiency and inner strength, she was determined to rebuild those qualities in herself. Alone. Slowly. Carefully. She had in mind a cautious wade back into life.

Mike's kiss had been the shock of total immersion, a slam of life, a surge of emotion. He was a man to make a woman forget rhyme and reason.

But not you, Carra. That's exactly what would always make him the wrong man for you.

She put him determinedly out of her head. All she had to do was stay out of his way and do her job. Of course she'd be nice to him, but she'd simply avoid all private personal contacts....

She could easily do that. She was more than ready to sleep on that thought, when a drip of water splashed on her forehead. Her overtired imagination? Her eyes blinked open. A second fat drop splashed on her cheek, then another. Then a thin, long stream of them.

The roof leaked.

Mike had established routines for dealing with insomnia. Over the years he'd tried late-night movies, walking, whiskey and the Blonde. The Blonde worked best. Past midnight he was already halfway through the daydream seduction—the Blonde was already bare, willing and *lush*—when he heard the faint knock on his door.

The first spare knock upgraded into a relentless pounding and rattling. He reluctantly pried his eyes open, tugged on jeans in the dark, ducked for the killer bedroom arch and went to save his door. A simple turn of the latch did it.

The reason why the Blonde wasn't denting his insomnia that night had exchanged her traveling outfit for a red angora sweater and jeans. Nothing much else had changed. Her skin was still a faultless porcelain, her blue eyes still fringed with black lashes, her legs still dangerous to a man's blood pressure.

She was lovely as sin, and he saw right off she was working up to a Boston-proper conversation. God knew how long she'd been standing there, but rain glistened in her hair like diamonds. She held herself defensively erect, arms wrapped around her waist and shoulders as rigid as his slide rule.

"I'm terribly sorry to bother you. Believe me, I wouldn't have if I could have avoided it."

He could see that. "Would you get in here before you're soaked?" He guessed they were going to pretend the kiss had never happened. Once he closed the door, there was no light beyond the banked fire in his fireplace.

"I love the cottage, but I'm afraid my bed's as wet as the Atlantic. The roof leaked. It happened so fast I couldn't stop the bedding from getting soaked. There weren't any spare blankets, so I tried curling up on the couch using clothes for cover, but it's an awfully small couch. I thought perhaps you might have a second blanket you could loan me."

He couldn't help being aware that she avoided all eye contact, all body contact and particularly any view that included his bare chest. "The only blanket I have is on my bed, but it's warm and dry. You're welcome to camp out here for the night."

She hesitated. "I wouldn't dream of putting you out of your bed."

"Good," he said dryly. At two in the morning a man didn't dither. "The bed's big enough for two, whereas the couch is two feet shorter than I am, and I'd have a real hard time getting excited about sleeping on stone floors."

"I never intended—"

He knew what she'd "never intended." She was tense as a cat in a downpour. "We'll have your roof fixed in the morning. Actually, it would have been done if you hadn't arrived early. I had a couple men scheduled to give your place an overhaul before you got here, but that's spilled milk now. You need a shot of whiskey to sleep?"

"I—no, thank you."

"Tea?"

"No, but thanks."

"Fine." He couldn't help a giant yawn. "So it's already halfway to morning. Catching sleep time. Unless you have another idea?"

Silence reigned for a lengthy two minutes. He didn't need a doctorate in psychology to know she hadn't come over here to share a bed. In principle he wasn't any fonder of the idea than she was. That kind of closeness would put his hormones through torture.

Hormones, however, were temporarily the last thing in his mind. She was exhausted—pale-white exhausted, soft-eyed exhausted, unable-to-think exhausted. Someone needed to haul the woman to bed, soon, and he'd do it if she didn't stop dawdling. Then she surprised him.

"You're right. It's past sleeping time." She hesitated again, and then faced him with a briskly cheerful smile. "If it's all right with you, I'll take the door side instead of the window."

Men his size didn't take sides; they took up an entire bed. But he didn't mention that, and instead he simply led her through the low-hanging archway to the bedroom. "You want a T-shirt? Something to sleep in?" he asked matter-of-factly.

"I'll be fine."

"Hmm." Since he'd never turned on lights, his eyes were already accustomed to the darkness. He shrugged off his jeans, took the pillow nearest the window and waited.

He heard her shoes drop to the floor and, in due time, the scrape of her jeans' zipper. She stripped off the pants but was still wearing her sweater when she edged down on the mattress. When she slid in, her knee touched his; she jerked hers back. When he tossed her half the quilt, she jumped. But thankfully, the lady was too darn tired not to settle in pretty fast.

His eyes closed, but not from sleep. The scent of wet roses seeped through the crack in the window. Her perfume was more elusive than ever, though it hinted of fragility and spice.

He mentally tried to recall the fragrance of the last woman who had driven him out of his mind, but couldn't because there *was* no woman who'd driven him out of his mind.

He'd loved more than once. He always fell in love the same way—hard, violently, totally. When a man gave that much, he always got something back, even if the love affair didn't work out. Mike never worried about forever. He worried about the here and now of life, wringing the most out of each minute, stealing the best out of each day. He loved big, he lusted big, and he roared into emotions with everything he had.

And at the moment he felt something like an ox trying to sleep next to a rose. Carra avoided touching him ever so carefully. Hours before she'd more than touched him. She'd surged in his arms and yielded like a princess just wakened, a lover come to life. Instincts of protection and cherishing had been swamping him.

They still were. Ten minutes passed, then twenty. He banished mental images of her bare thighs and soft mouth. He thought of the sadness in her eyes, then banished that thought, too. Tomorrow he'd figure out Carra O'Neill. The lady desperately needed rest. To make sure she had that rest, he recounted football scores.

"Mike?"

He pried open his eyes most unwillingly.

"You're not asleep, are you?"

Not now, he wasn't.

He heard her head turn softly on the pillow. "It matters a great deal to me that we get along. I just want you to know that I've completely forgotten about what happened."

It didn't quite sound that way to him. "Be kind of silly to wage war over a single kiss," he murmured.

"Of course it would be."

"We're square again?"

"Definitely."

"So let's get some sleep."

His lids drooped down again. Football scores weren't working. He tried sheep. All the sheep in his head wanted to discuss spring and mating seasons. Every one wanted to know what life wounds had built the shield around a raven-haired woman with mystical blue eyes. Every one of them wanted to guard her, cuddle her close, make absolutely sure she was warm through the night.

Still, he'd had a sixteen-hour workday before he'd met her. Overworked muscles wanted to relax. Overstressed limbs wanted to grow heavy....

"Mike?"

His last prayer of a peaceful night's sleep dissolved. He flipped on his back, turned his head. "Irish, you are *dead* tired," he informed her.

"I know. I just didn't thank you for offering me a bed."

"Half a bed."

"Whatever. I owe you."

"We'll discuss payment tomorrow."

"I also want you to know—what's wrong?"

He'd leaned up on an elbow, all snapping, awake-dark eyes and a looming scowl. "Look, Carra, you're not only beautiful as hell, but you're half naked in my bed. I know what you want. To hear out loud that you're safe. I can't give you that written guarantee unless you help me. Dammit, go to sleep!"

Dead silence. Frost collected on her side of the bed. "This is ridiculous. I'm getting out of here. I really don't see that there's a chance on earth of our working together."

"Damnation!" He jerked to a sitting position and reached for the bedside lamp. The light momentarily blinded both of them. "Are you deliberately trying to drive me out of my mind, woman?"

"Me? Of all the nerve—"

"We're going to sit here and talk this out. Reasonably," he roared.

Reasonably? Carra knew better. His copper hair was as wild and disheveled as any ancient Pict warrior. Tufts of more hair coated his chest. His shoulders were as big as a freighter. It was perfectly obvious to her that she was in a situation that she couldn't, wouldn't and didn't even want to handle. Retreat might not reflect valor, but it tasted a lot safer than this. "There's nothing to talk out. We obviously have a major personality clash going on here."

"Nonsense!" But his voice abruptly softened. He plopped both their pillows against the headboard, and then settled, knees raised under the quilt. A wayward grin suddenly replaced the glowering frown. "A bed's the best place I know to settle differences."

"Not in my book, Fitzgerald."

"Maybe you've been in the wrong beds?"

The expression in her eyes abruptly turned livid. "See? That's exactly what I mean. There's obviously no talking to you."

"Would you listen?" But for a moment he was hard pressed to talk. Her arms were folded across her chest, her eyes snapping dares and she was bristling with anger. Something simply got lost between her fury and his eyes. She was so soft, so small, so damned exhausted that fragile shadows wreathed her eyes. "Look," he said firmly. "Let's not imagine problems where there aren't any. I have a job to do at Glencorrah. So do you. We both want to be here, and as far as I can tell we both share a mutual respect for each other's commitment and qualifications. What better basics could two people have for an excellent working relationship?"

"In principle that's true," she qualified.

He nodded. "So the only problem is that I got slightly out of line and threw a small pass. Irish, the Lord could look at you and throw a small pass. What's the big deal?"

The backdoor compliment put color in her cheeks. "*Nothing*, as far as a kiss. Look, Mike, try and see it from my point of view. I just traveled across the Atlantic. I'm alone in a foreign country. My one main contact for the next two months is you. If you're not going to keep your hands to yourself...."

He nodded. "You're right. I see your point."

"Good."

"And all you want to hear is that I'll keep my hands to myself, and we're all set?"

"That would help." Her tone was as dry as fine wine.

"Can't do it."

"I beg your pardon?"

"I said I can't do it, Carra." He shook his shaggy head ruefully. "The way I see it, you wouldn't be still sitting in this bed if I seriously threw you for six. You're of age; you're sure as hell not scared of me; and you liked that kiss."

"If you're not going to be reasonable—"

"Reasonable's easy. Honesty's tougher...but much more interesting." He thumped the pillow and settled lower. "I can pretend I'm not interested. You can pretend you felt nothing when I kissed you. It seems pretty silly, though. Attraction is not a worldwide crisis. It's natural. If worse comes to worse, all that happens is that we go through the usual things men and women go through. I try; you say no. I pursue; you defend. I show up with champagne and moonlight; you counter with your best right hook. People have been having that kind of fun for an awfully long time. No one can work *all* the time. What's the big problem?"

The immediate main problem was that he was giving her a headache between his languid grin and the leisurely lecture. In fact, she was sorely tempted to put her head in her hands. Glencorrah was her bid to get her feet wet in life again. Mike was like immersion in the ocean without life rafts or buoys. "Look, I'm *trying* to be seriously honest with you. I don't play. I *never* play. Not those kinds of games."

"You don't play games. You don't believe in the little people. You don't believe in romance. Irish, we're talking some serious lacks in your life-style." He reached up and flicked off the light. "We'll finish this discussion tomorrow. I hate to be the one to mention this, but you're half zombie."

"I—"

"You're going to sleep. Right now."

"But—"

"*Sleep.*"

The damn man. He turned on his side and lay there like an immovable tomb. Bare minutes passed before his breathing evened.

Tense, tight and irritable, Carra slid back down under the quilt. Sleeping was out of the question. Before morning, long before morning, she had to figure out how and if she was going to be able to manage working with Micheal Dougel Fitzgerald.

She meant to think. She *had* to think. The courage it had taken her to come to Glencorrah only stretched so far. The work in itself was a monumental challenge for a woman who'd lived on self-doubt for two years. She'd counted on her love for Glencorrah to help carry her through. She'd counted on that safety and security of history to use as ballast, determination, the push to get her life moving again.

She had *not* counted on a Pict-Irish devil named Fitzgerald.

You'll never sleep, she warned herself wearily, yet promptly felt the thick wool of wild, deep dreams taking her. Foolishness. She imagined herself held, warm, safe....

Three

***

Kisses. Without opening her eyes, Carra stretched long and lazily, still not believing she'd wasted an entire night dreaming about kisses instead of Glencorrah and Ireland. Disgraceful. More disgraceful yet was the sleepy, tingly feeling of well-being seeping through her limbs and consciousness. Sleep was its own salve, and for so long her dreams had been shadowed by mistakes and dark corners.

Her eyes opened, abruptly trying to absorb sunlight, the slovenly late hour and the slanted-ceiling charmer of a bedroom. Mike's stamp in the room was unavoidable. His leather jacket hung on a hook. A fisherman's sweater peeked out of a half-open drawer. And he'd pinned a note on the pillow next to her.

The Pict was a scribbler. He also clearly woke up in a sassy frame of mind. The note announced he was gone, which she had already, thankfully, realized.

Apparently, he spent part of each Monday in Limerick, giving progress reports to Mr. Killimer, their mutual boss. In the meantime, she had permission to raid his refrigerator for breakfast, and she was not to worry about her cottage. Today he would have the roof fixed, the amenities checked, some food stocked. He wanted her to put her feet up and relax until he returned.

And cats can fly, hmm? So all right, Carra, go get your feet wet at Glencorrah, but do yourself a favor and avoid Sean McIllenney until I'm back.

Mike hadn't signed the note, but there was a post-script. The next time they slept together, it said, he intended to make sure she had no time, opportunity or occasion to snore.

She crumpled the note, feeling both amused and bemused. So many orders! Such arrogance! Mr. Fitzgerald seemed to be under the insane impression he knew her very well.

A whimsical sensation of softness tried to drift somewhere near the vicinity of her heart. She banished that feeling. Mike didn't know her, and it was better that way. She thought of the clutches of guilt and battles for self-respect, which had dominated the past two years. Mike had only met the surface Carra the night before. Her problems weren't his. She would be very careful it stayed that way. In the meantime she had very obviously slept untouched, untroubled and unbothered.

You sure talk a lot, Fitzgerald, she thought. All baggage. You're not half as disturbing or dangerous as you let on.

She flew out of bed, feeling a rare, lovely, powerful sting of vitality. Maybe Mike was part of it. Maybe his kiss the night before had rubbed a little Fitzgerald-flavored arrogance off on her. She felt just a little arrogant, a little plucky and a whole lot determined.

Glencorrah was waiting. Ireland wasn't Boston. Ireland gave her purpose, energy, possibilities. Ireland was a place where a woman could put the past to bed, grow, learn, thrive and maybe even come into her own again.

She was counting on it.

Four hours later she'd lost all her arrogance, most of her pluck and was seriously considering checking out the plane fares back to Boston. Ceaseless noise and flying debris greeted her as she paused at the archway to the west tower.

At this height a wild, lonely wind blew off the Shannon River. A scaffold surrounded the tower where a parapet was under construction. Masons were laying the last of the wall near the arch. Drillers were fashioning windows in the breastwork of the parapet, and a crane was hoisting a clawful of stone block from three stories below.

Holding on to her hard hat, Carra picked her way through the noise and debris toward the brown-haired man flinging orders from the top of the scaffold.

The working set of blueprints under her arm were her own. The hours of comparing the plans to the reality of Glencorrah's keep and baileys, kitchens and towers had been pure joy. The seep of history had captured her senses; the sounds of construction had fired her enthusiasm. Castles were peppered all over Europe. None compared to Glencorrah.

Nothing had prepared her for the reception she'd gotten from the castle crew. Yesterday Mike had hinted the boys had a slight animosity toward a woman on the construction site.

Direct animosity, however, had been her last problem. Everywhere she'd turned, there had been musical brogues and charming grins. The devils were darlings. Right up until she tried to ask a direct question about the castle construction progress.

In principle, a medieval historian didn't know how to run an earth mover or need to, but Carra's job had two dimensions. A living museum called for a live cast; her major time commitment this summer was to train a self-sustaining tourist staff to act out the part of fourteenth-century characters.

The reason she'd arrived midway through construction, though, had nothing to do with training the staff. The castle's foundation was done, the construction projects were down to the last nuts and bolts and finishing details. The historical accuracy of details was her other bailiwick. Neither a foreman nor an architect nor a carpenter had any reason to worry whether the archways were constructed of ishlar or limestone. Mr. Killimer, her boss, did. And so did Carra. Compromises between construction techniques of the fourteenth and twentieth centuries were inevitable, but when a judgment call was possible, Carra was hired to represent the historical authority.

Representing authority was possibly her last goal in life, and bossing people around had never been her cup of tea. But she had counted on a little cooperation. Compromise and judgment were going to be a teensy bit tough if the Irish lads were determined to treat her like a cotton-fluff pariah.

Heading her worry list was the foreman of the construction crew, Sean McIllenney, who seemed to equate meeting her with catching the plague. Every corner she turned, he was miraculously gone. Every room or tower she entered, he had just left.

She'd finally caught up with him now, because she had to. The choice was either making peace with the foreman or heading back to Boston. Heading back to Boston was beginning to sound infinitely preferable.

Sun glared in her eyes as she neared the edge of the parapet. "Mr. McIllenney? Sean?"

"Yeah, yeah, yeah. What now?" The man whipped around, his eyes narrowed. His face was shadowed by the construction hat, but every inch of his exposed skin was covered with grime. From dried mortar-covered jeans to work boots, Sean McIllenney was a chunk of lean-muscled toughness. "Mother Macrae, I thought you were Carney!"

"No." She tucked a strand of hair behind her ear and tried her most professional smile. "I'm Carra O'Neill, and I can see you're in the middle of work. I don't want to bother you. I just wanted to ask you to schedule a minute when you've got the time."

He gave her a moment's shrewd, measuring glance. "Now's as good as any time. Wait there." He barked something to the men below, climbed down from the roof edge and strode toward her. His swagger was distinctly macho, but there was a faint grin when he stopped in front of her, glanced at his palms and shook his head. "Haven't got a hand worth offering a lady."

"Nonsense." She firmly extended her own. He wasn't tall; their eyes met on a level, and at a glance she guessed his age to be around thirty. His skin was burned to the rough red of roof tiles, and he had sun-glinting, blue hawk's eyes. His grip was gritty, dusty, quick. The handshake had nothing of Mike's power and warmth. It possessed a lot more than the hostility she'd been expecting.

"Killimer made real clear we were to wait on you hand and foot when you arrived, and Mike said the same thing this morning. Crew said you'd been wandering around."

"Yes, everywhere. I'm impressed; you've done a terrific job. And I certainly don't expect to be waited on hand and foot, but I do need to sit down with you when you have a free minute—"

"Like I said, now's fine. Haven't had a break in hours. Come on, we'll get you out of the wind and dirt." He motioned her through an archway to an inside tower room, cleared off a carpenter's bench and abruptly straddled one end. "Now, lass, first things first. You got a problem, I want you to know that's what I'm here for. No need bothering Fitzgerald or Killimer."

Surprise nearly tied her tongue. Perhaps all her shaky hands were for nothing. "Mr. McIllenney—"

"Sean. Make it Sean."

"Sean then." She tugged off her hard hat and wished she hadn't. His eyes immediately followed the fall and tumble of her hair. She took a breath. "For several months I've had two sets of blueprints to work with—the original fourteenth-century plans for Glencorrah and the current working blueprints. I see a lot of changes—"

"There always are, lass. Reality is always different than paper and pencil ideas. Nothing was changed that didn't have to be."

Carra differed. Rather drastically. She'd seen nothing on her four-hour tour that had been architecturally changed, just bits and pieces that were different. For example, the location of the main kitchen well and the moat depth weren't accurate, and a right-sided staircase in the north tower that should have turned to the left. Maybe the changes had been structurally easier, but they weren't right. Not fourteenth century right.

Carra wasn't about to make snap judgments, and the last thing she wanted to do was wage a war with Sean on first meeting. She did need to find out how he was going to be to work with.

She opted to try out the most mild red herring on her list. "Castle defenses are a favorite of mine, Sean. Maybe that's why I particularly noticed the breastwork in the gateway tower."

"The barbican?"

She nodded. "I saw what you did with the murder holes and arrow loops. They're just right, but what happened to our gun holes?" He raised an eyebrow; she forged on. "It probably seems like a silly detail. And it would be, since guns were rare in Ireland for another several decades, but this is Glencorrah—state of the art for its time. Crossbows wouldn't have been the only hand weapon used by a defending knight."

"Our knights would use a few guns, hmm?"

"All day. And if they used guns, they needed a hole to aim them through, especially on the lower walls and barbican at the gate. I'm almost certain several Bodram gun holes were inked in on the working set of blueprints." She was dead sure. "Any idea what happened to them?"

"Can't imagine."

"Is it going to take some kind of horrible, major correction to still put them in?"

"Not at all, not at all," he assured her blandly. "An oversight, that's all it was. You didn't bother Mike with an itty-bitty problem like this, did you?"

Her brows lifted. "Truthfully I haven't seen him all day. Even if I had, this hardly seemed an architectural issue. If you'd rather I took things like this to Mike—"

His brogue was as thick as butter. "Just the opposite, lass. Mike already made real clear what you want is what you get. You're our authority on stuff like this, aren't you? You just bring these kind of problems to me; I'll take care of them." He swung a leg over the bench and stood up, reaching for his yellow hat again. "Now, what else can I do for you?"

"Not a thing, immediately." Her shoulders lifted, tension gone. Relief danced in her stomach, and her smile was radiant. He'd listened. All right, maybe gun holes weren't of earth-shattering importance, but a dialogue had been started. After the way the crew had treated her earlier, she had been terrifyingly aware of how difficult her job would be without cooperation from the construction foreman. "I need to see and study a lot more before I could give you a decent list, Sean. Maybe if you could schedule a spare hour or two by Thursday."

"Thursday's just fine, but I have an immediate, better idea than that." He doffed the hat, looked at her. "Course, you'll probably take it the wrong way...."

"Try me." He had to be joking. She'd be happy to do cartwheels if she thought they would help establish a decent working relationship with this man.

"Well...I just thought...see, there's this pub in town, maybe not as fancy as you're used to, but they serve a good Irish stew. Not to misunderstand, I've my lady in Kilgeggan, but eatin' alone's no fun, and a shared ale's a good way to talk out any ideas you got on your mind."

She hesitated. His gaze beat steady on hers, so steady that for some reason she felt uneasy. It's just paranoia, she mentally scolded herself. Caution had become a habit. Once guilty of bad judgment, she was wary of making another mistake. *And I just don't want to make a mistake here, at Glencorrah. It means so much.*

Yet, already she'd let caution talk her into misjudging the attitude of the work crew, and she'd anticipated a hostility from Sean that had not proven out. So now, was she ready to close up because she imagined a suspicious glint in his eyes?

"If you have some problem with the idea of dinner—"

"No, not at all." *O'Neill, you have to get over this overcautious nonsense.* The better she knew the man, the easier working with him was going to be. She threw warmth in her voice. "Dinner sounds terrific."

"Say tonight around seven?"

"Couldn't be better."

"It sure couldn't," drawled a lazy tenor from the doorway. "In fact, a dinner tonight will give Carra a good chance to meet a few other members of the crew at the same time. I'm sure that's what you had in mind, wasn't it, Sean?"

"Mike, you belong in a cave." Carra crossed her legs, fussed with the cuff of her blouse and watched the rolling hills dart by.

"Still irritated with me, are you?"

"Irritated? Of course not. I'm delighted to go to this bar and have the chance to meet the crew in casual and comfortable circumstances. The more, the merrier." The clasp loosened on her bracelet. She reclipped it, then discovered a crease in her print silk skirt. "I just couldn't understand your attitude toward Sean."

"He's a damn good foreman, but there was also a reason I suggested you avoid him until I got back."

"Yes, you keep telling me he has a little prejudice against women. I think you're suffering delusions." Somewhere in her purse was a tiny mirror. She certainly didn't want to walk in with smudged lipstick. "He went out of his way to listen and be helpful. He didn't give me any reason to think we'd have a problem working together."

"No?" The tone of Mike's voice was mild. He hadn't felt half so mild on walking into work that afternoon. Laughter and money had been changing hands. McIllenney had taken one look at Carra and bet he could have her alone and in bed within twenty-four hours. Men's locker-room talk was predictably more boast and bravado than reality. Mike had given the boys a fast dose of reality even before he'd found Sean with Carra. "Tread carefully with Sean, Irish," he advised lightly.

"I was and I will. Try and believe I've worked with men before, would you? Successfully. No problems." Her blouse collar itched. She fixed that, and then folded the black knit cape closer around her. The temperature was dropping as fast as the sun.

"Men in academia could be slightly different than the breed in a construction crew."

"Fitzgerald, we need to get off this track before I bop you one. I am not naive. I do not need a resident bodyguard, and I've dealt with awkward situations before. Your men are not going to get any encouragement from me. Am I getting through?"

"What did you talk to Sean about as far as work?"

"Micheal!"

"Oh, God. Not that schoolmarm tone again."

She sighed, loudly, which earned her a chuckle and a fast grin. For a fleeting moment her eyes squeezed closed. Shakespeare's Kate had protested too much. Maybe, so did she.

The need to share with Mike the crew's lack of cooperation and her uneasy feelings about Sean was all too tempting, but she couldn't. Glencorrah was a test for her—a test of self-sufficiency and pride, a chance to prove to herself that she could trust her own judgment again. No one could help her pass those tests. Running to Mike was out of the question. "How far is it to this bar?" she asked abruptly.

"You've got about five more minutes to fidget and fuss. You look edible now, Carra. More lipstick isn't going to change that, and there's nothing to be nervous about."

She opened her mouth with a fast retort and then closed it. *Edible*. Lord, he was sassy. She had to do something about that very soon, but for now she'd just sit back and watch the gold-tipped hills streak past. Occasionally she caught the glimpse of a thatched-roof croft, a shepherd herding lambs, black earth just turned that day.

The catch on her bracelet slipped again. It always did; she didn't know why she even put it on. She pulled the offending jewelry off altogether, stashed it in her purse and heard Mike's irrepressible chuckle. "I'm not nervous," she said flatly.

"I can see that." He murmured, "Just be yourself, Irish. I promise it'll all come out right if you just be yourself."

He was dead wrong. Mike couldn't know that "herself" was a woman capable of making terrible mistakes. Carra didn't want to be *herself*. She wanted to be a stronger, better person, the kind who could handle herself in any situation, a woman who never slipped up because of emotions.

She was trying, but several things were making that immediately tough. Walking into a bar full of men struck her as being as much fun as chicken pox. An awareness that this could turn into a test of her acceptance was enough to cause her hives. And sitting so close to Mike had her heart tripping erratically.

She sneaked him another critical glance. He drove with the same laid-back easiness he did everything else. The rangy shoulders were contained in an innocuous gray shirt; his copper hair needed a brush. His eyes looked a little tired. For the dozenth time she tried to convince herself that he was just a man.

And "just a bar" loomed ahead of them. She could have missed the whole town on a blink. There was nothing but a church, a country store and a bar, all built in the same fieldstone that dominated the countryside.

The church and country store were deserted. Vehicles clustered around the lights of the little bar. Red Hugh's said the sign, and abruptly her car door opened.

Mike's grin was as lethal as the devil's. "No time to take a nap now, Irish. They're just good old boys, I keep telling you. And I'm going to be right there."

"Honestly!" She climbed out, feeling bristly and . . . worried. She would have removed his hand at her back if it hadn't felt like such an anchor.

The bar was crowded. Three dart games were going on simultaneously, and a roaring political debate raged at the bar. Beefsteak and oyster puddings were the advertised specials, posted with a thumbtack on the wall. Most tables had a pitcher of ale as a centerpiece.

Possibly the Irish didn't allow women in their battered sanctuaries, because the only woman Carra saw was the aproned redhead carrying a tray. The rest were men, all ages of them, most dressed in rough jeans or serges, all built tough and dark and wiry. Lilting brogues and raucous laughter diminished as Mike led her through the room. Carra's palms turned wet. None of the eyes fixed on her were hostile; it was just that there were so many of them.

Mike's hand gently squeezed her shoulder as she sank in the chair. "Obviously you know Sean. And you must have run into our two Gerrys today—Mannion and O'Hara. Gerry M's our chief carpenter, and there's no better mason in the business than O'Hara. Gallagher here doesn't do much, but he'd like to have us believe the project wouldn't survive without him. Water's his business, as in moats and wells and drainage; he'll talk your ear off on the subject if you let him. And don't let any of them start on politics or we'll be here all night. I can't believe you four polished off the first pitcher without us."

Mike tossed his jacket and her cape somewhere. The house specialty was ordered and she managed to identify each man. Gerry M reminded her of Al Capp; Gerry O'Hara blushed like a beet when his name was mentioned; Gallagher had hard eyes and a defensive tilt to his shoulders. None of them looked as if they wanted to be here—at least now that she'd arrived—and Mike didn't help matters.

"Killimer gave you clout, Carra, but he never backed that up by explaining exactly what your job is to any of the crew. Why don't you tell them something of your plans, while I get us another pitcher."

So easily, so deliberately, he wandered off. How could you, Fitzgerald? she thought.

As soon as he deserted her, silence hovered at the table. It wasn't a friendly, companionable silence but a tense one. The men at the table were sitting as rigid as schoolboys at an unwanted lecture—except for

Sean, who sneaked her a wink and a nudge of his knee.

"Well now . . ." Sunburst had nothing on the smile she tried. The only other choice seemed to crawl under the table.

If her job meant any less to her, she wouldn't care about what they thought. But Glencorrah meant a great deal. A little hesitantly, she started by explaining what a living museum was—a chance for people to see, taste, touch, hear and smell the fourteenth century firsthand. "That's what's so special! No display tables, no off-limits roped-off rooms." Once her tourist staff was trained and the castle was open, tourists would be able to talk to knights and pages and stewards. They'd be able to taste roasted boar, see what was planted in a castle's gardens, discover how and why an armorer made a castle's weapons. "Armor, tapestries, crossbows, wimples, cooking utensils, bedding—those kind of details are my job. To make them right, to make them as carefully authentic as I can."

Silence. For a moment she was almost certain her own enthusiasm had caught their interest, and then Sean cleared his throat. Abruptly Gerry M chewed on a hangnail. Gallagher made eyes at the buxom redheaded waitress. Mr. O'Hara was fascinated by the foam on his beer.

Wading through snow in bare feet would have been easier. Since enthusiasm had bombed, she tried a basic dose of sincerity.

"I keep hearing that Mr. Killimer made a point of my authority. Look, I find that whole business awkward and don't mind admitting it. I'm not here to get in anyone's way, but to offer help when I can. What I'd like to do is pool resources, share informa-tion...."

More dead silence. Then Mike arrived with the beer, the redhead brought dinner, and the boys dove in.

Two hours later Carra threw herself into the car and closed her eyes with her head against the backrest. Mike started the engine next to her. "Gosh, that was fun," she said dryly. "The last time I had that much fun, my brother locked me in a closet with a garter snake when I was eight years old."

"Nasty brother."

"*He* shaped up over the years."

"The crew gave you a pretty hard time, didn't they?"

"Hard time?" She deliberately kept any hint of ac-cusation from her tone. "Pity you played darts after dinner. You missed the real interaction. Gallagher said 'thank you' when I passed the bowl of peanuts."

"I deserted you for a reason, Irish."

"Who's complaining? You're entitled to play darts, and this was my problem, not yours." She turned her head. "I *did* have the rather nasty feeling that the boys had made up their mind about me long before I got here."

"They did. And whether you know it or not, you handled them perfectly, did exactly what you had to do to turn that around."

"You must have been gone longer than I thought. I didn't handle them at all, Mike. Didn't you notice?"

Unsmiling, Mike shot her a glance and noticed any number of things. Her breezy humor only worked so far. Her face was ghost-white, and her eyes luminous with stress. He also noted that she hadn't protested his desertion in the bar. Carra O'Neill wasn't looking for a knight to handle her battles for her.

Still, he'd never met a woman who needed one more.

Not you, Fitzgerald, he reminded himself. All through the drive to Limerick and back, he'd repeatedly told himself the obvious: he'd just met Carra. He didn't know her well enough to form a serious, honest bond of caring. A man who'd been alone a long time could be prone to overvalue, overimagine, overneed the emotions that came with a commitment to a woman.

The pep talks were worth the hole in a doughnut. He looked at her and felt something special. A kindred loneliness, a matching pride, a fierce feeling of protectiveness and the obvious—desire. It all added up to dynamite. Dynamite that was igniting at a miraculous rate, simply sitting in the same car with her.

"I hate darts, always have," he mentioned.

"Pardon?"

He said quietly, "I left you alone with the boys for the simple reason that you were nervous and showing it, Carra. They needed to see that, needed to know that you were a nice, decent lady instead of a brassy Yank looking forward to threatening their jobs." He took the first left turn. "We'll leave out Sean's role in how and when and why they'd formed those preconceptions about you. What matters is that they met you; they could see you weren't the bossy bitch they were expecting."

"But—"

He didn't give her a chance to finish. "You were never going to overturn Rome in a day, but whether you believe it or not you did terrifically. And your working with them will do the rest. Give them a little time." He glanced at her. "And give yourself a little, too. You just got here."

He'd given her a lot to mull over, but none of it changed how badly the last two hours in the bar had gone. "I do wish you'd told me more about what I was getting into before we walked in there."

"And worried you more than you already were?" Softer than a whisper, he murmured, "Dammit, who slammed the confidence out of you, Carra O'Neill?"

"I didn't hear you."

"It was nothing. Let's go."

Rather belatedly she noticed that Mike had braked to a stop, but not in the driveway to their cottages. "Go where? Where is this?"

"A good place to walk, and it's definitely walking time. You can't sleep on stress; I've tried."

She considered arguing until she stepped out of the car.

The night was ebony black, but not in this moonlit haven. The roll and pitch of the road through the hills had led to the Shannon River. The river glowed under moonlight with the serenity of a mirror, currents softened by night, the shoreline silver-tipped and still.

Her shoes sank in the mossy grass; the smells were sweet and heady and fresh. Far across on the other side she could make out a single tower standing tall and shadowed and white, glimmering in the reflection of the moonlit river. She looked at Mike.

"I don't know what the tower is. Some ruin of some abbey sometime. Somehow these things endure. You can't drive anywhere in Ireland without running across a rain-worn castle or a fallen nave or pagan stones strewn around. I think the little people protect them."

She gave him a wry look, but he was dead serious. He pointed to a small rise of land a few hundred yards in the distance. "See that?"

"The little hill?" She didn't see anything else he could have meant.

"Our destination. And it's not a little hill, it's a mound. The Irish call them 'raths', and raths are traditionally fairy forts."

"I see," Carra said dryly.

"Regrettably we're not likely to catch any fairies at this hour. Twilight's the magic time. We're late, but you can't come all the way to Ireland without sitting on a rath."

"Ah."

"Do I keep hearing the Boston twang of skepticism?"

She chuckled. "I'm a realist. I did warn you."

"I know you did, but luckily the problem's curable. Just come this way, coaxed the spider to the fly."

She laughed again and was suddenly aware how long it had been since she'd laughed, really laughed. She told herself that she was crazy. The problems of her job were real, and the nature of those problems festered around the whole arena of judgment that most worried her. She should be feeling an anxiety crunch. She should be frantic.

And she was, for a time, but the mood refused to hold. It wasn't a long walk to his little grassy mound. Tension slipped away with every stride.

The whole sky was a polka-dot fabric of stars. Scents hovered over the green fields and gorse, wistfully sweet scents, as fresh and soft as yearning. The air was a life-celebrating cool. She could taste the stillness. The peace was free.

Mike climbed the knoll ahead of her and, at the top, sank down to the grass and motioned her to the spot next to him. "Now, sit. And try not to relax. You'll see it's impossible."

"Because of the fairies?"

"Of course, because of the fairies. Now close your eyes and give it a try."

She sat, closed her eyes and tried not to relax—and discovered not relaxing was impossible. The little people had nothing to do with it; it was just that kind of night.

"I knew you'd like it," Mike murmured with satisfaction.

She opened her eyes and focused on him—really focused on him—something she'd carefully avoided doing all evening.

He talked a lot of nonsense, but she was just beginning to understand that that wasn't the real man. Mike's easy, lazy ways hid perception and intelligence. From big, bold shoulders to the lines on his face, his body mapped some rough, traveled roads. He knew what he wanted. Mike was the kind of man who would always know.

The barest breeze ruffled his hair, and even sitting with his legs sprawled, he cast long shadows in the moonlight. He could have been a Viking Pict survey-ing the land he intended to conquer in battle. Unfor-tunately his eyes were dancing with possessive pleasure over her face, not the land. "I love it," she said mildly. "And I would love it even more if the only reason you brought me was to show me a rath."

"Why else would I have brought you here?"

"To make a pass, Fitzgerald." Schoolmarms had a way with a certain tone.

"God, the distrust, the lack of faith, the cynical wariness." He shook his head. "Of *course* I brought you here to make a pass, Irish. You're beautiful and this is moonlight."

Slowly, lazily, he eased her down. His arm made a pillow; his long thighs made an anchor. The grass was damp with river mist; she would have been cold with-out her cape. She wasn't cold, because of the cape, and also because Mike radiated more body heat than a fire. But she didn't let Mike know that.

He'd touched something in her from the moment she met him. Something unexpected, unwanted, dis-turbing. She couldn't defend herself from an enemy that made no sense. That he'd met her and formed an interest hardly mattered. Mike had been stuck on the construction site for months, so anything in skirts would probably have set his hormones in motion. His attraction couldn't have disturbed her less.

Her own attraction disturbed her a great deal. Months of celibacy had added up to two years since the baby died. She'd never missed a flesh-and-blood man, never gone looking, never worried about that lack in her life. She'd had opportunities. None had tempted her. There had to be a rational explanation why Mike was different.

She saw his eyes just before his mouth softly brushed hers. Dangerous eyes, she thought dispassionately. Dangerous eyes that teased and wooed with promises of short-term madness.

She felt the feather of his breath before his lips claimed hers a second time, slow, lingering. His kiss was a giving. That was another danger, she considered logically. Most men took with a kiss. Mike knew enough to disarm a woman; next time she would remember that. All it took for a woman to win all her battles of survival was knowing the enemy, arming herself with the appropriate defenses and having the patience and inner strength to withstand a siege.

Mike, amused, tasted her cool, smooth lips again. So limp, so unresponsive! He guessed he wasn't supposed to notice that her pulse was racing, her body braced with tension and that the small hand at his shoulder—prepared to push him away—was trembling.

"Open your mouth," he murmured. "Now, Carra."

She didn't want to.

Sleek, slow, he let his fingers play over her face, slide into her hair. His kiss nuzzled and coaxed until her lips parted. The inside of her mouth was dry, but not for long. His tongue dampened, tasted, explored, until the small hand at his shoulder tightened into a ball.

An emotion shook him, deep and strong. He'd wanted to move her. He wanted the anxiety gone from her eyes. He wanted the wariness she felt around Micheal Dougel Fitzgerald permanently erased. Why it mattered so much, he didn't know and didn't care. It mattered.

But Carra—when her lips finally yielded beneath his, when her throat arched, when she suddenly surged toward him with something of wildness and something of anger and something of helplessness— threatened his sense of gravity. Her mouth was sweet, vulnerable. She smelled like roses. He sensed heat and softness in the cold black night and felt this woman's priceless, defenseless need. The fire was so fragile. It was as if she didn't know passion, wasn't expecting it.

He wasn't expecting the surge of tenderness, the lush emotions of power and protectiveness, the fierce, huge need to simply love her. He knew instinctively that she needed kisses. She needed light and brightness. She needed someone to be there, and that need was raw, inexplicably new and frightening to her.

Need was nothing to be afraid of. He showed her, whispering kisses over her porcelain throat. His fingers found the edge of her cape and slipped in. His hand was huge, her breasts small...small and swollen and aching-warm for the slightest graze of his fingers.

He caressed her breasts and ribs before allowing his hand to slide down to her hips. Her skirt was silky, soundless beneath his fingers, and the feel of her hips sent desire shimmering through him like a lost summer wind, hot and strong.

She wrapped him close, mindlessly, her mouth returning pressure, her limbs trying to curl around him. She'd forgotten that the grass was damp or that the air was cool. She'd forgotten completely that she'd fully intended to knock his block off if he tried a second pass.

"Irish," he murmured softly.

"Hmm?" His cheek had a night-beard roughness. Where he rubbed her throat, she felt like shivering all over.

"If we take this a minute further, sweetheart, you're going to be naked. And so am I."

She froze, fast, but he was already fastening the catch at the throat of her cape, withdrawing long kisses in favor of short ones. Possessively he pushed down her skirt, finger brushed her hair. Her eyes had the glaze of a woman coming out of shock, and not a nice shock.

Unsmiling, his gaze wandered over her face, her flushed cheeks, her unsteady lips. Moonlight painted her face white. Whatever she wanted or didn't want, her stress seemed all out of proportion for a woman who had to have been kissed before, loved before, known passion before.

"Amazing, the power of the little people, isn't it?" he murmured idly. "These raths in moonlight cast a powerful spell. You didn't believe me, did you?"

She couldn't talk, not just then. She was still trying to assemble the cause of her crazy, leaping heartbeat, the reason her lungs couldn't remember how to haul in air. It had nothing to do with Irish fairies and moon dust. She knew that.

But that she could be forming feelings for any man—and especially this man—was just as impossible. She didn't care for Mike. She couldn't. She didn't know him well enough to care for him. And not once in many years, had she considered that passion could take her like magic, the rush immutable, her common sense left trampled and defenseless.

Carra knew herself well. She had every reason on earth to be absolutely positive that none of these things could have happened.

But they had.

Four

The entire ride home, Mike watched nervousness build in Carra like wax collecting around a hot candle. Still, she waited until he was stopped in front of the cottages and the car key pocketed before she laid her hand on his arm. "Look," she said. "I'm asking you to leave me alone."

He liked the honesty, no frills and no excuses. "You're not married," he said with quiet sureness.

"No—"

"A lover at home?" He phrased it gently. He didn't want to give her the impression he was going to buy an immediate ticket to Boston to murder the man.

"No, that's not—"

He enclosed her hand, lifted it and let his thumb move slowly down the pulse of her wrist. "We didn't make love, Carra. We didn't even go halfway. All that

happened was a special moment in the moonlight—
and it *was* special. For you. For me. I don't know
about your life, but I know about mine. That kind of
specialness is too damn hard to find.'' He released her
hand and reached for the door handle. ''I'm not married. Never have been.''

''I didn't ask you that.''

''I'm no woman's knight. Have no illusions there.
But I was also never a tomcatter. I was raised in a loving family, and it's a loving family I want. I had a
couple of relationships when I was too young to know
what to do with them. And one long love affair in the
recent past.''

As soon as she climbed out of the car, she slammed
the door and glared at him over the hood. ''Micheal,
I don't want to know. It's none of my business!''

He rested his elbows on the car top and leaned forward. ''Of course it is,'' he corrected her peaceably.
''I'm coming after you, sweetheart. Obviously you
should know what you're getting into. I have a slam-
fast temper, but no woman's seen it or ever will. I can
cook when I have to, no drinking problem. I tend toward protectiveness; I guess that's kind of annoying,
but I'm as faithful as a sheepdog and expect the same.
As far as qualifications as a lover—''

''Good Lord! Would you stop it?'' She leaned her
chin in her hands. Disastrously, his boy scout list of
virtues almost made her want to laugh. Maybe if his
gaze was less intent and probing across the distance of
the car, she would have. In the dark, his eyes picked
up the luminous glow of the moon. ''Mike, you don't

need to tell any woman your qualifications as a lover.
You are one. But I'm not looking."

"Neither was I. Until you crossed the Atlantic."

"But I'll be crossing back—"

"So will I. But not for another couple months.
Long enough to figure out how big a problem Boston
to California is going to be."

"That isn't going to be a problem."

"I don't think so, either. California's never been
more than my token base, because I've hop-skipped all
over the place with my work. Even before Glencorrah
I decided this was my last long-term traveling expedi-
tion. I'm tired of camping out. How bad are the win-
ters in Boston?"

She said patiently, "You're going too fast."

"Always have. On the other hand, we could immediately drive to another fairy rath. You could teach
me to take it nice and slow. I could practice..."

"*Would* you listen?"

In his own way he had been. Her changes of
expression, her eyes, her hands had all been telling him
stories. Now, though, he waited and watched her take
a long breath, a frantic one. Words spilled out of her,
raw and catching, clearly nothing she intended or
wanted to say—but that was why he'd been gently,
teasingly goading her. To catch that honesty.

"I'm trying to tell you that I'm not looking for a
relationship, not with you, not with anyone." She
swallowed, and then snapped it out. "I was unmar-
ried and pregnant and lost a baby two years ago."

She saw his face change expression, his eyes deepen
and darken with compassion. She looked away.

"That's not your business or your problem, Mike. I'm only telling you so that you'll believe that I mean what I say. Nothing's been the same for me since then. The kind of person I thought I was doesn't seem to be at all the person I've turned into. I *need* to make changes, need to get on with my life, and I took on Glencorrah to try again."

"But work is all you feel you can handle right now?"

She sighed. Maybe he did understand.

"You've been down a damn tough road," he said quietly.

"So has everyone," she said. "That's no excuse for the mess I got into. I chose my own roads, just like everyone else. And just like everyone else, I have prices to pay for making a wrong turn. I have to do that alone."

"Why?"

"Why?" She shook her head. "Come on, Mike. There are things everyone has to come to terms with alone."

It was perfectly obvious how totally she believed that. Unmoving, still, his gaze fastened on her face. He never raised his voice, but from nowhere his tenor turned fierce, butter with an edge, silk with a sharpness. "Where the hell was he, Carra?"

"What? Who?" His question seemed out of place and context.

"The man whose child you lost. You haven't mentioned him once, which pretty much says it all. He wasn't there for you." The last was a statement, not a question.

A knife twisted in her stomach. She ignored the old sharp pain, stiffening from both old habit and pride. "He has nothing to do with this. I only told you about what happened to explain; I don't want—"

"To love again. To feel again. That isn't what you said, but believe me, I heard you." Before he could change his mind, Mike strode around the front of the car, captured her hand and walked with her to her cottage door. The kiss he dropped on her forehead was as fleeting as dew and just as fragile. "I'm sorry you've been through hell. Not a little sorry, not polite sorry, not I-don't-know-what-to-say sorry, but from the pit of the gut I-mean-it sorry. And if I did something to bring on those tough memories, I never meant to. You're special and you're beautiful—"

"Mike—"

"And you're going in your own cottage, alone and now, to sleep. At seven sharp I'll bring over breakfast."

She had barely stepped inside before he'd closed the door and ordered "Lock it" from the other side. For more than a few seconds she stood immobile, bewildered. One minute they'd been talking, and the next he'd trundled her out of his sight faster than Cinderella's fairy godmother.

It wasn't midnight. And she wasn't through with the conversation—nor did she intend to be—until she was absolutely sure Mike stopped the flirting game, the pursuit-and-capture game men and women had been playing through the millennia.

Slowly she peeled off her cape, then headed for the bedroom to pull off clothes. The day had been long and emotional and disturbing. Micheal Dougel Fitzgerald had come closer to her in two days than she'd let anyone in two years. How could she have told him about the baby, when she'd told no one else? And how could she have so totally lost her head on his moonlit 'fairy rath'?

Impatiently she thumped the pillow and curled under the quilt. She knew exactly why Mike drew her to him. To pretend otherwise was silly. He listened, made her laugh, made her remember how good it was to share. He was big and lusty and natural. He touched her, and she felt so irresistibly special. So special that the earth moved and she was tempted to believe in forever afters again.

Once upon a time she'd believed in gallant knights and forever afters. Not any more. Of course she wanted to love and be loved, as long as romance didn't clutter up the emotion. Hormones were like rhinestones, fake glitter. Being wooed was a heady rush. Moonlight and champagne encouraged a woman's fantasies.

Carra had been down the whole damn road. Drowning in duck soup was more fun, and Mike scared her. She was a realist now, immune to the temptation of romance, no longer susceptible to those kind of idealistic fantasies.

Only she didn't feel much like a realist when he held her.

Carra closed her eyes. She couldn't repeat old mistakes again. For his sake as well as hers, she was not meeting him for breakfast in the morning. She was not roaming any more "fairy raths" with him. And she intended to get very skilled, very fast, at staying out of Mike's way.

Mike pushed at the lace curtains, checked the two parked cars in the driveway, and then glanced at his watch. It was three minutes after eight o'clock. Seven minutes since he'd looked the last time.

The sun was setting. A windswept Monday was nearly over. And she still wasn't home.

For an entire week he'd practiced patience. A good man didn't pursue a lady like a buck in heat. A good man didn't bully a woman into talking about the damned bastard who'd deserted her while she was pregnant. A good man gave a woman time and opportunity to develop trust.

The marines needed a few good men. Mike wasn't going to make it on the list. *Where are you, Carra?* He jammed his hands in his back pockets and glared at the window. He'd had a very long week to find out exactly what her habits were.

Mornings she spent chasing down the road at killer speeds. Killimer had given her a list of locals to check out for her potential tourist crew. She was accumulating her tourist crew. She'd also collected two seamstresses, an old priest who wanted to help her set up the chapel and an ancient lady with a love of Irish history.

Afternoons were her castle time. Finding her then was a question of catching her. She was as likely to be cutting oiled screens for the keep's window as trailing tape measure and blueprints through wet mortar with the masons. The boys claimed she could climb a scaf-

fold faster than a cat. He'd personally seen her testing a ballista crossbow more than half as big as she
was.

Evenings she fixed a quick dinner, and then walked.
Those long walks, he guessed, ensured that he didn't
casually walk next door.

Regardless, she was always home by six. It was now
eight-thirteen. Tired of pacing, he stalked to the bedroom, tugged on his work boots and headed back for
the window again. *She's in trouble, Fitzgerald.*

The thing was, what kind? All week he'd watched
her grapple, test, and then immerse herself in a job she
obviously loved. He'd already guessed Glencorrah was
some kind of monumental test of confidence for her;
he had yet to understand why. Initiative, motivation,
expertise, capability—he'd seen it all. She was doing
more than fine. Her jean-clad hips were gradually
picking up a cocky swing; working alone, she was inclined to hum.

She also had a secret vice. If he hadn't insisted she
share the office space in the solar with him, he would
never have discovered it. Carra was a closet thrower.
Her real love was Styrofoam cups, but pencils and
shoes ran a close second. The first time he'd come
across an oddly disheveled office, she'd been scrambling, fast, to right things. Now he measured her
frustration level by how pin perfect he found the office. If he found his pencils lined up like soldiers, he
figured she'd housecleaned to hide her vice.

The slight quirk in her character touched him. So
did her dominant stubbornness at never asking anyone for help. She *was* doing fine, but that wasn't to say

her days were running smooth as glass. McIllenney's boys were giving her a rough time. He expected McIllenney was giving her more than a rough time, but Carra never admitted it.

She hadn't avoided him. The opposite was true. Mornings, she had a smile and a sparkle and fresh coffee waiting for him in the solar. More often than not, he forgot a sandwich at lunch. She inevitably tracked him down, nudged a sandwich in his hand and found a place to sit cross-legged while she coaxed him to talk about his day's frustrations.

The damn woman acted like his best friend.

She didn't seem to understand that her actions were like throwing bait to a bear. The sizzle of chemistry alone would never have sustained his interest. She was warm and sensitive. She was funny, smart, proud. And she was vulnerable.

Too damn vulnerable, he thought. Now where are you? He checked his watch. 8:45 p.m.

Abruptly he knew where she was. There was only one place she'd go if she were in any kind of trouble. From the day she'd arrived, he knew the keep had special meaning for her. The keep was the strongest, most defensible holdout in any castle, and from Carra's viewpoint, stone was a marvelous medium. It weathered storms, time, generations. Stone protected and endured.

Unlike men.

He was halfway through the door when he stopped, stalked back to the kitchen ell, foraged for the bottle of wine he'd bought three days ago and headed for the door.

* * *

"Mike!" Carra had been so lost in thought that she hadn't heard the sound of any footsteps. One minute she was alone, and the next he was standing in the doorway, his hair windswept, tarnished copper and his cheeks ruddy from the chill night. One look and her heart picked up the rolling beat of a bluesey torch song. Not now, Fitzgerald, she thought helplessly. Being around you all week has put my peace of mind on the endangered species list. But I don't have time for that now.

"I had no idea you were here." Mike's brows raised in shocked surprise. "If I'm interrupting something you're doing—"

"No, of course not." She scrambled quickly to her feet and started scooping up wads of paper balls. "What brings you here this late?"

From the look of a trash can brimming with paper basketballs, she'd had a hell of a day. The white pinch of stress around her eyes underlined the fact. He pushed off his jacket, damning himself twice over for not finding her hours sooner. "Nothing, really. Often enough I just walk here evenings. Our cottages are a great size for a woman—or a man with stunted growth. If head-bumping claustrophobia doesn't get to me, insomnia inevitably does." He raised the wine bottle. "Share a glass of wine with me?"

"If you're looking for a little peace and quiet, I could just as easily clear out of here."

"Actually, I'd appreciate the company."

When Carra hesitated, he took advantage and poured two Styrofoam cups of wine. One look at her and he wondered what miracles had allowed him patience this long. The fisherman's sweater buried her breasts, yet it somehow made her figure look regal and long-throated and Boston fine-boned. Her jeans were loose, yet demurely snugged at her fanny and teased at the shape of her long, slim legs. And her soft, blue eyes shimmered with anxiety.

He lifted the cup toward her and mentally crossed his fingers that she felt differently about wine than whiskey. "I shouldn't," she insisted. "I haven't had dinner yet."

"One drink won't kill you, will it?" He tried his most boyish grin. "You can't make me drink alone after a day like this one."

"You had a rough day?"

"Wicked." There, he had her. Her fingers closed on the cup, and concern immediately erased the private anxiety in her eyes.

"What happened, Mike?"

He pulled up the stool and droned on about a water-table problem affecting structural tolerances.

He was still embellishing the tale when he dipped the wine bottle into her cup a second time. She didn't seem to notice. He noticed a great deal. She was gulping the wine as if it were soda pop, but it took the second cup before even the palest rose colored her cheeks. How much wine was it going to take to loosen her tongue?

Perched on the cot, her back snuggled to the wall, Carra kept promising herself she would leave as soon as she finished the cup of wine. She'd hoped some brooding hours in the refuge of the keep would offer her answers to a witch of a day. It hadn't worked. All she'd done was stress herself out on a nasty anxiety trip.

Mike's wine was settling in her empty stomach like rolling, warm honey. No more, she warned herself, but Lord, she was tired. She was tired of worrying about her judgment and tired of being careful. A night wind from the open window made the lantern flick wild, ghostly shadows on the castle walls. Lonely shadows, until Mike had walked in. He needed someone to talk to. Was that so dangerous?

"So you got it solved?"

"Finally." Quieter than a cat and just as deliberately, he leaned forward with the wine bottle again. She was too busy looking at him, too busy listening, too busy trying to look as if the world hadn't caved in on her, to pay any attention to the amount of wine in her cup. "And you've been letting me ramble on all this time," he chided her lightly. "Don't try and tell me nothing interesting happened in your day."

She tucked her legs under her. "Today had a few glitches," she admitted cheerfully.

"Such as?"

"Nothing, really. Sean threw me a little curveball." A quick frown puckered her forehead. She'd particularly never intended to mention Sean to Mike. The room was suddenly so *warm*. She pushed a strand of hair behind her ear, adding quickly, "Nothing I can't handle—also nothing I shouldn't have expected. Not worth a discussion, Mike."

He figured it was. He also considered for several seconds what kind of man would sneak wine on a woman who was obviously no drinker. That answer was obvious. Lazily studying the soft flush of color on her face, he felt only nominal guilt. She was talking. Or would be soon. "Now don't ask for help, Irish. The walls might cave in."

She chuckled, but insisted, "This isn't something you or anyone else can fix. It's something I have to."

"So tell me what you need to fix."

He coaxed and pulled until he had the story. Last Thursday she'd met with Sean to give him the list of construction issues she needed help with. She needed a catapult and trebuchet built. The main doors to the keep required a certain kind of lock and jamb to be historically accurate. The kitchen required a beehive-shaped baking oven of a certain depth. Her list went on, nothing that sounded so terrible or major to Mike, but for Carra the whole thing broke down to some kind of "gun hole" she wanted in the barbican tower.

"Sean not only promised he'd jump on my list," Carra said wryly, "he went out of his way to be encouraging and cooperative, and just like fish for a worm, I bought it until six o'clock tonight. I've been so busy, and it was really the first chance I had to make a progress tour."

"He hadn't done anything?" Her eyes were getting a sleepy glow, like a woman's eyes when they softened with passion. Mike sent two wrenches, a carpenter's belt and a weight measure to the floor. The cot sagged when he dropped next to her, knees up, back against the stone wall. He brought the wine bottle with him. When she raised her cup for emphasis, he tilted a little more brew inside.

"Mike, he'd done *zilch*. To an extent, I understood. He certainly has other priorities besides mine. But the boys were finished up on the barbican yesterday and now their stuff is cleared out, which made it pretty darn obvious he'd never intended to drill my gun holes."

She pushed at her hair, leaving a flop of bangs standing straight up. He wanted to kiss her. He particularly wanted to kiss the finger she was wagging at him. "Don't you dare interfere, Fitzgerald. If you jump all over McIllenney, I'll be stuck hiding behind your shoulders everywhere I turn. He'll never listen to me."

"You're right," Mike agreed.

"I have to find a way to get along with that man."

"Yes." A barest smile touched his lips.

"It was a first skirmish. I lost, hands down. In principle, I suppose I could have taken my darn list to you or Mr. Killimer, but that would have meant going over Sean's head. And these were construction issues. Not your problem."

He hated to interrupt, but had to. "McIllenney reports to me, Carra, for a reason. My name gets stuck being attached to the finished project of our monster here. That means I have a need to know any problems going on."

"*You* don't have any problems with Sean. I do. It's perfectly obvious he's a good foreman—"

"His boys would walk on water for him," Mike agreed.

"So it's me, not him. He took one look and decided I was a doormat. How can I work with a man who thinks I'm a doormat?"

"You can't work that way," he agreed.

"I have to tell him off."

"Yes."

She waved the cup for emphasis. Lord, she'd worried about this problem for so many hours. Why? Nothing, suddenly, seemed so hard. The room was toasty, the wine was wonderful, and Mike had soft, warm, magical green eyes. "I have my own authority. So what's wrong with using it? All I have to do is make it clear that I won't tolerate those kind of shenanigans ever again."

"Yes."

"Mike?"

"Hmm?"

"Why are you smiling at me? Nothing's funny here."

He memorized the label on the wine bottle before filling her cup again. "I might have been smiling, but I wasn't laughing at you, Irish. I was admiring you. You know exactly what you have to do, and you're going to do it."

For the third time she tried, unobtrusively, to ease away from any physical contact. That was hard since there was a natural slide down to where Mike sat. It came from his weighing somewhere near two hundred pounds and her tipping the scales at almost a hundred pounds less. Where the sizzle between his thigh and hers came from was another story.

Regardless, she'd been almost sure he'd offer her an argument, not agreement. It could be she'd been harboring a few errant daydreams about Mike pinning Sean to the wall. By his ears.

"You think I should give him a little hell," she said cautiously.

"Yup."

Yup. Again Carra pushed at her hair. The thought gave her ulcers. She never gave people hell; she reasoned with them. She didn't yell effectively. She aspired to power not at all. She'd never successfully told anyone off in her entire life. Tough just wasn't her style.

"Look, Irish, if you want me to take him on for you—"

"No." Men weren't knights in shining armor; she wasn't a damsel in distress. This was real life. McIllenney was a turkey, and besides, the idea of Mike admiring her had aroused her pride. He didn't seem to feel any doubt she could handle McIllenney alone.

"If you run into trouble—"

"No, no. I'll handle it."

"I know you can, and well." He rolled his shoulders against the stone wall to appease an itch. Someone was going to get blamed for her headache tomorrow morning. Somehow, he didn't think the little people would take that responsibility. "Let's make a deal, Irish. From now on, you save a few minutes at the end of the day; we'll talk. You keep me informed, and I promise not to interfere unless you ask for help. Fair?"

"Fair." But her mind had drifted away from the subject at hand. Through the window she could see clouds scuttling past a huge silver moon, but that view couldn't hold her attention, either. Mike's left hip had all her attention. It snuggled against hers, hard, muscular and distinctly arousing.

He had a runner's long legs, tight hips, and where his jeans stretched near the zipper... O'Neill! she cried to herself. Get your eyes away from there!

She did, although she didn't move terribly fast. She didn't much feel like doing anything fast. Her limbs felt sleepy-loose, her mind was fuzzy and her blood seemed to be dawdling up and down her veins. Mike had a wonderful body. All week long she'd been reading herself a riot act any time her eyes wandered anywhere near that body.

Silliness. Sexual feelings were delightful, delicious, powerful. Amazing, how clear her mind was suddenly. There was no danger in wanting Mike. Any woman would *want* Mike. The danger Mike presented had nothing to do with sexual need, but other needs.

A woman's need to be held could be terribly... annoying. When she was anywhere near Mike, she was tempted to believe that he was a man to hold a woman when it mattered, when it counted, when a woman felt scared and small and...

"I *have* to go home," she said abruptly. As soon as she lurched to her feet, the castle walls started weaving.

She touched her fingers to her temples, and suddenly Mike was there, threading her arms through the sleeves of her jacket, smoothing her hair. "Something is wrong," she said vaguely.

He knew. His laggard sense of honor was the main thing that was wrong. He had no moral problems with using wine to coax Carra to talk. That first cup of wine, though, had guaranteed she was safe in his care.

Darn morals. Her face was tilted up to his, all sleepy blue eyes and parted lips. Her mouth was yielding, soft. He wanted to take it. He wanted to take a hell of a lot more than her mouth.

The capacity for passion was in her eyes, so was a vulnerability and loneliness. The expression on her fragile features was so naked he felt the air slam out of his lungs. This was how she could be. This was what he needed from her and what he wanted for her.

But not because of wine.

This was the last time she was getting any liquor from him. None of Ireland's best, and *never* wine.

"Micheal—"

"Yes, we're getting you home, sugar. Believe me, faster than you know."

Five

Morning sun bathed the courtyard in the color of pale honey. Six hundred years before, Glencorrah's knights might have gathered outside the bailey on a morning like this, weapons idle as they listened to their lord's battle plan.

Standing at the fringe of the crowd, Carra's hands were slung in her pockets, her expression bemused. The twentieth-century knights wore hard hats and suspenders. Their weapons were drills and saws and earth movers. Mike led the group, as he did every morning. He wore no armor, but his height and physical strength and clear, powerful tenor unmistakably identified him as the castle lord.

When the boys had straggled into the yard, most of them had been sleepy and yawning and half awake. By the time Mike finished with them, they were back slapping and jostling each other, ambition in their strides and purpose in their expressions.

Mike had said that the boys would walk on water for Sean, but Carra thought ruefully that he was the one with the charisma. He had the boys believing they couldn't wait to sweat under a hot sun. And he'd had her guzzling wine the night before like there was no tomorrow.

Her head had a lot in common with steel wool this morning. Her scratchy mood did not improve when the yard roared into life. Truck engines started up, and a bulldozer revved next to her ears. Over two dozen heads, the devil caught her eye, gave her a fast wink and motioned toward the far side of the scattering crowd. She understood: Mike had searched out Mc-Illenney for her.

How nice of him. Walter Raleigh had sacrificed his coat for a lady. Mike would probably expect the lady to carry him over the puddle.

Maybe she didn't believe in knights and chivalry, but she was hard-pressed to remember how he'd talked her into a showdown with Sean. She'd been a timid mouse in her personal life for the past two years, afraid of her own judgment, afraid to get out there and take a chance. Granted, she'd come to Glencorrah to change that around, but it didn't have to be this morning. What was wrong with a week from Thursday?

Mike was still looking. Hands still slung in her pockets, she forced her scratchy mood and pounding head across the courtyard. Regrettably, she didn't realize a half-dozen men were clustered around Sean until he spotted her. Immediately he pushed back his hard hat, jammed a knee forward, hooked his thumbs in his belt loops and smiled.

There were smiles and there were smiles. Sean's specialized in patronizing arrogance. From wet palms to the sick knot in her stomach, Carra was strongly inclined to head back to Boston. She would have, if it weren't for that damn red-headed Pict. The wine hadn't clogged her memories of Mike last night. He'd had the nerve to believe in her. He'd had no doubts she could handle this.

And because of Mike, she cleared her throat and said firmly, "I need to talk to you."

"Sure thing, lass." He glanced at his boys; they didn't move. They also didn't talk, although conversation died like a fly for a swatter, leaving Carra to believe they were all on to the little joke Sean had played on Glencorrah's medieval historian. "You come across another little construction problem for us, did you?"

The boys thought that was funny. Carra felt a cup of emotion start to simmer in her stomach. Maybe it wasn't courage, but it was darn close to anger. "Would you mind telling me the status of that list we talked about?"

"All those projects are pending, Miss O'Neill."

"Like the gun holes were pending when your men were conveniently working in the barbican? You're all finished there now."

"Completely, lass."

She'd been sure he would at least offer an excuse. That he didn't bother showed exactly what a frumpy doormat he thought her. Well, isn't that what she'd been lately?

But that wasn't how Mike saw her. Mike took a problem and shook it from the rafters. He *liked* problems. He saw life as a brazen challenge to have a good time. He seemed to think she shared his opinions.

She tucked her fists on her hips and tried lifting her head with a little borrowed Fitzgerald arrogance. "You did a great job of making me look foolish, Sean," she said lightly. "Maybe I would have done the same thing in your shoes, if some stranger walked in here with a fancy degree and started slinging orders. Who says I know what I'm doing?"

His smile froze in a classic mug shot. He started to say something, but Carra figured her run on courage might not last too long. Besides, in for a dime, in for a dollar. "You doubt my competence—that's fair. But I'd at least like a chance to change your mind, prove what I can do. And I believe I can do that, if you'll loan me a drill, a chisel and a pair of safety glasses."

"A drill?" he parroted. He appealed to the others with a look to share the humor.

"A drill. The Bodram-style gun hole I wanted for the barbican tower—I'll drill it myself." The idea appeared to startle him, but not half as much as it had startled Carra to hear the words pop brazenly out of her mouth.

"Mother Macrae, you couldn't weigh seven stone. You couldn't even lift one of our drills."

Six onlookers had propagated into an even dozen. Her heart was thumping louder than a 747's engine. "They aren't easy to handle, are they?" she agreed. "I spent a summer several years ago on a road crew. The boys used to call those drills 'boulder busters,' probably because holding on to them was like riding a bronco. I'm sure not saying it was my favorite job, but I managed. If you're afraid I'll ruin your wall—and I'm sure you are—you can give me a test run. Find me a slab of concrete, and I'll show you exactly what I can do.''

"You'll break your neck, that's what you'll do! And I don't care what your Yank crews do, it's different over here. You think I'd let a bit of a *caillin* anywhere near any of my heavy equipment—?''

His macho stance hadn't changed, but she seemed to have done something to dent the ice chips in his eyes. What it was didn't matter. There was honest concern in his voice, and suddenly there were only two of them there and to heck with the crowd.

"Sean, I need everything done that was on that list," Carra said quietly. "If you really can't bring yourself to cooperate with me, I'll find some way to do it myself. In fact, that's what I'm trying to tell you. I'm going to do my job, with you or without you, but if you have some problem working with a woman—''

"Who said I had any problem working with a woman?''

"Well then, you must have taken a personal dislike to me on sight—''

"Mother Macrae, I never disliked you!''

"If I offended you in some way I'm unaware of—''

"You haven't done a darn thing to offend anyone!''

She shrugged her shoulders, offered him a grin. "Then why on earth are we having a war? Come on, McIllenney. Let's start this whole thing over with a handshake."

When Mike heard Sean yelling something about Carra breaking her neck, he felt an itch that started in the palm of his hand and spread through his fingers and arms. Carra looked as fragile as a wildflower in the growing number of male bystanders. In any decent fairy tale it was the exact moment when the knight would come charging in on a white steed to save her from the dragons.

Skip the dragons. Mike would have settled happily for knocking McIllenney on his keester. Sean was an outstanding team player, a leader with his men, a competent, ambitious, knowledgeable foreman. In short, he was an architect's dream of a co-worker, but McIllenney had a hard head where women were concerned. A bit of a black eye might help rearrange his thinking, and Mike wouldn't have minded delivering it.

He couldn't, because of Carra. She had to know she could handle her own. She needed to win. He knew that with the instinct of a man who'd waged his own battles with courage and confidence. And he knew it as a man who cared about the lady with the raven hair and far-too-pale face. Mop him up, love, he mentally urged her, and then, finally, he saw Sean throw up his hands.

He couldn't hear what was said, but he saw Sean gather up Carra in a back-thumping hug. He heard the boys' roaring laugh of approval. The group dispersed. Sean still had an arm thrown around Carra's shoulder as they went off.

A gun hole miraculously appeared on the west barbican wall before eleven. By noon, Carra was sharing a sandwich and coffee picnic-style by the riverside with the crew. Mike watched her in consultation with Gallagher after lunch. Sean joined in that conversation, his look as protective as a hen for his favorite chick.

That was when Mike stopped being pleased about how well she'd succeeded in charming the boys.

For the next seven days she gave him daily reports about what she was up to. For the same seven days Mike listened like a mentor and behaved like a monk. It wasn't easy behaving like a monk, because it was during that week that he fell in love. Not a nice, easy, dawdling trail into that state of emotion, but a fall like a clunk—hard, irreversible, painful.

Watching Carra come into her own was watching the heart of a woman come to life. It was a big heart, a sensitive, warm, loving heart. But her gift of giving was aimed in the wrong direction.

She was as obsessed with the castle as if it were a lover. She behaved as if working on it could keep her warm at night, as if caring for stone and mortar could give her loving back.

Stone and mortar couldn't, but by the following Thursday Mike decided that Carra's passion for castles could be used to an advantage.

If a man were sneaky enough.

No construction noise penetrated the thick stone walls below ground level. If the keep had any ghosts, they belonged here. The air had the thick, dank smell of a place that had never seen sunlight. The underground rooms were brooding, dark and as small as cells, with only small, narrow windows placed high on the walls.

The chill had penetrated Carra's light red sweater when she first walked down, and that had been an hour ago. Even absorbed in thought, she heard the quiet clip of a footstep from the top of the stairs. She guessed it was Mike before he rounded the corner, ducked for a low ceiling arch, and stopped dead with a low, rolling chuckle when he found her.

"I have to say, it's a miracle I found you. I checked the solar, the kitchens, the north tower, the moat crew—all your favorite hideouts this last week. What are you doing down in the dungeons?"

"Thinking," she said wryly.

"It's a good place for it." He glanced around. "Also a good place for spiders and rats to find their own."

"It does have a little Frankenstein atmosphere, doesn't it? But never mind that. Since you're here, you can sit yourself down and help me solve a problem."

"What problem?"

She motioned to the wrought-iron bars on the narrow windows. "The boys and I are having a little war about those bars. See, this isn't really a dungeon."

"Could have fooled me."

"That's what the boys say." She'd picked up the Irish gesture of throwing up her hands. "In reality, though, castles didn't have dungeons. They had *donjons*, which is just another word for keep. Traditionally the rooms down here were used for storage, and that's why they were cold and dark, not because they were dungeon jail cells. Riffraff and prisoners were never kept here but in the gate house—the only logical place where a castle would have regular guards on duty.''

She paused on a mellow sigh. Mike had crossed his arms and was directing one of his patient grins at her. He had a habit of doing that whenever she went off on a history tangent.

She would be much less inclined to go off on a history tangent if Mike were a smaller man and if his eyes weren't an unholy shade of green. She'd babble less if his smile didn't remind her quite so much of the pagan genes in the ancient Picts.

How long had she been working with him? Long enough to know Mike was a special blend of brick, boss and ballast. It may not be wise to trust the devil, but he'd given her no choice. They'd spent hours together. He'd never once pushed a pass—not even the night he'd encouraged her with the wine, not once since the evening she'd told him about the miscarriage.

He'd given her nothing to worry about, except her pulse rate accelerated to the speed of sound whenever he was in the same room. Also, Mike sometimes had a way of looking at her, as he was now, that made her think of nasty things. Lying naked beneath him. Passionate kisses. Demanding lovers. Stars exploding and slippery sheets.

She thought ruefully that her feelings for Mike had a lot in common with chicken pox. The doctors claimed most people were immune after the first case, but you really could catch it a second time. This time, Carra kept telling herself that she knew better, but the problem was Mike. He wasn't like other men. He was bolder, stronger, sexier and, God knew, sassier.

"Wipe the grin off your face, Fitzgerald. Darnit, I had to give you the history background in order to explain. I've been arguing with the boys about those window bars for two days."

He rubbed his finger on the bridge of his nose. A few weeks ago, the idea of "arguing with the boys" would have made Carra anxious. Now she sounded like she'd been handed a Coney Island hot dog heaped with relish.

"The boys know dungeons are *donjons*. They know the bars are wrong, but they want them on anyway. They claim every tourist from here to Siam wants to see an honest-to-God awful, dismal, spooky dungeon and to heck with realistic history. So what do you think?"

Her eyes were a dancing blue. The skinny, red sweater accented two small, plump breasts, and the denim work skirt hid far too much of her legs. Mike figured, though, that Carra really didn't want to know what he thought. "You're willing to let me cast the deciding vote?"

"Certainly. As long as you make the right vote."

"You wouldn't be trying to tie my hands, would you, Irish?"

She propped her hands on her hips. "All right. I swear to heavens you men all think alike. I'm perfectly capable of taking a crowbar to those window bars myself."

He let out a roar of a laugh. "Just like you're capable of handling a 'boulder-buster' drill?"

A flush skimmed up her cheeks. "You heard about that, did you?"

"Nine times, each time embellished with more detail."

"The full truth," she said firmly, "does not always serve. I *did* work on a road crew my sophomore year in college."

"Pushing paper?"

"Pushing reams of paper. The closest I ever got to one of those drills was to get a number on it for parts." Her lips started twitching when his did. "You tell McIllenney and I'll never forgive you. After all, when in Ireland, do as the Irish do. This *is* the land of sweet gab and blarney."

"Exactly."

She blinked. "Exactly what?"

"We're finally getting to the reason I tracked you down here in the first place. I'm about to steal you away for the rest of the afternoon on a matter of critical importance."

"Critical importance?"

"Research," he said gravely.

She couldn't get a clue out of him for an entire hour and a half drive. By the time he parked and she realized their destination, she couldn't believe it, or him, even after she'd climbed out of the car. "This is the *research* you had in mind?" she demanded. "For this

I left hours of serious work, responsibilities, a half-dozen unfinished projects—"

"You're going to love it."

"Mike, it's a tourist trap."

"Nonsense, it's tradition. How can you be a history lover and not respect tradition?"

"Mike—"

He'd waited a long time to kiss her. Too long. Her breath shortened when he ducked his head and silenced her list of objections with the warmth of his mouth on hers.

Her heart gave a bronco buck. Heat and ice shot through her veins at the same time. The rogue had given her absolutely no reason to expect a kiss. His lips were as warm as sunlight. His hands clutched her shoulders, kneading softly, urgently. She could feel the impatient tension in his thighs...and then he broke away, his wayward grin instant, fat, dark lashes shielding his eyes.

"Behave," he ordered her.

"Me?"

"We're going to kiss the Blarney stone, and I don't want to hear any more objections from the Peanut Gallery."

"Call me a Peanut Gallery again and watch how hard a big man falls." The threat made him laugh. Her knees were quaking. The kiss had been quick, nothing that necessarily crossed the line into a woman's emotional danger zone. There was no real sizzle in the air. The green lawn hadn't suddenly turned emerald, the sky bluer, his eyes a more intimate golden green.

I don't need you. I can't need you, Mike.

She forced her attention away from his face. Surrounded by lush pastures and green woods, Blarney Castle's main tower thrust high and tall against the sky. Ivy crept up the rough gray stone as far as the eye could see. "If the Blarney stone's at the top, we have a heck of a long trek."

"We're going all the way, Carra. Don't doubt it."

Her eyes whipped to his face, wary of the innuendo. He just grinned and draped an arm around her shoulder. "Take it easy. We'll take those steps slow and one at a time. In the meantime, try to control yourself."

"Control—"

"I know you're all excited. Nothing like battlements and parapets to bring out the passion in you, Irish. And once you've kissed the stone, I have in mind the most dangerous dinner you'll ever have or hear of."

"You've already kissed this stone, haven't you? There's no other excuse for this steady stream of blithering."

"Blarney? A few generations back, my relatives were all from the county of Cork. The gift of gab comes naturally."

There was admission to pay, but amazingly no other tourists were crazy enough to waste a Tuesday afternoon on such nonsense. They practically had the castle to themselves. Inside it was dark and cool, sunlight shunted out, the scent of history invading the ancient stone walls. The self-contained stairway leading to the top battlement was circular, winding to the right. It had no foyers, no chambers or anterooms, no rest spots. After the first thirty steps Carra's knees, calves and arches begged for mercy.

"I can't."

"Of course you can."

Fitzgerald's favorite words where she was concerned. If the foolish man wasn't half so sure she could do any and everything, she would have faltered more than once over these past weeks. Still, there was a limit to the power of his coaxing. She looked up. "Exactly how many steps are there?"

"No more than a hundred zillion." He patted her fanny, urging her on. "Think of the knaves and varlets and brigands wielding swords on these steep stairs, fighting for honor, protecting the family virgins."

She droned. "Think of the five ton of armor they wore, their sore legs." After another thirty steps she stopped counting. Mike was the one to break for a rest, his lungs hauling in air as he rubbed his knotted thighs. "Give up?" she challenged him.

"Not in this lifetime."

"Try thinking about the virgins, Mike. And I know it's not as much fun, but then try thinking about honor."

"You'll pay for that sass at the top, Irish."

Finally they were in sunlight and on level ground again. Carra took a long draft of fresh air, saw the sign and crossed the stone floor to the edge of the parapet. One look and she firmly, violently shook her head.

The famous Blarney stone was attached to the external battlement. There was only one conceivable way to kiss it, by lying on one's back and being suspended in mid-air over the open parapet. There was nothing to hold on to but a thin iron railing.

"How many tourists have they lost, doing this?" Carra said wryly.

"None that have ever been publicized."

"That's supposed to be comforting?" But she peered over the side, drawn in spite of herself to all the lure and tradition associated with the famous stone. The rock was half her size, rough on the top, worn smooth as a mirror where thousands of lips had already kissed it. "Cripes! How unsanitary."

He roared laughter. "Where's my history lover now? A lot of famous men's lips have touched that stone, Irish. Lords and knights, knaves and priests and blue-eyed blackguards."

"Mike."

"Hmm?"

"Directly or indirectly kissing a zillion men's mouths has never been my goal in life." Strands of hair wisped around her cheeks from the soft spring wind. "I have a problem."

"Courage?" he teased. But he was wondering exactly how many men she *had* kissed.

"Courage is always a problem. But the more immediate crisis is my skirt." She motioned. She hadn't changed from her denim skirt when he'd dragged her off. She'd had no idea she'd needed to, and anyhow, there hadn't been time. The denim was serviceable and practical, but it was still a skirt. She wasn't about to go head down, legs exposed, wearing a skirt.

Mike's lips pursed in a sick attempt at looking seriously impressed by her dilemma. "And I'll be having to hold your legs," he said sadly.

"I'll hold my own legs. You hold my skirt down. With your eyes *closed*."

"Why, sure, Irish."

She sighed. He already knew she was going to do it. She guessed, so did she. "You're also going first. I'm not kissing this thing all by myself."

"No fun kissing anything alone," he agreed. He lowered himself down until he was flat on his back, then shimmied to the edge and grasped the iron railing. His head ducked down and out of sight. Carra held her breath, then he ducked back up again with a fast grin and a wink. "Your turn."

She would have felt less awkward if he'd moved a little distance away. He didn't move, and in spite of stockings and skirt and heavy wool jacket, she could feel his eyes taking intimate stock of her figure the instant he had her lying flat next to him.

Her fingers grasped the iron railing as his had. Where he'd had nothing else to hold on to, though, she felt the security of Mike's hands. Not at her skirt or legs, but on her waist, and wrapped tight so there was no potentiality of her falling. Wind combed her hair. For an instant, there was nothing between her and a five-story fall but an ocean of blue, blue sky and Mike's huge, strong hands.

She smacked the stone, feeling foolish. She thought of the vagaries of men who would think up such a custom, invest luck and hope and dreams all in the kiss of a stone. Then she thought of the vagaries of a woman, because she'd just kissed that same stone and felt a mystical brush of luck and hope and dreams.

Nonsense. She quickly pushed herself back, embarrassed to feel the slide of her skirt rippling up over her thighs. Mike only released her waist to capture her hands. He hauled her up, not just to a sitting position but to a standing one. Her cheeks were flushed, her eyes oddly bright. For that second he was standing closer than a lover.

"Well, we've done it. Once you've kissed the Blarney stone, aren't you promised the gift of eloquence for the rest of your life?" she said lightly.

"We'll find out for sure. In fact, we're going to test exactly how talkative it makes you over dinner, but first..." For the second time that afternoon, he leaned toward her, blocked sun and sky and wind and reshaped her mouth under his.

For the second time, she was not prepared. For the second time, his kiss was fast and fleeting. But it was very definitely different from the first. Now the pressure of his mouth was bold and firm, a rough claiming, a possessive stamp.

When he lifted his head, his eyes looked more gold than green, and his smile was gone. The pagan Picts had mercilessly strong bones, warrior blood, a love of the senses that had gotten them into endless trouble. Mike touched her cheek, and she felt a shiver. "That was for you, not me, Carra O'Neill. You were right. Too many other men have kissed that stone over the hundreds of years. Some of them had to have been black-hearted rogues, so you just remember that I kissed you last. We just erased all memory and contact with any other men's kisses for all time."

He never gave her a chance to answer, just talked up his "dangerous dinner" as a reward for reaching the bottom of those endless long stairs down.

Dangerous dinners didn't trouble her, neither did the fear of tumbling down the pit-steep steps. But Mike troubled her, because he was absolutely right. Every time he kissed her, she forgot any other man who'd ever kissed her, wanted her...hurt her.

Almost.

Six

———

I still haven't figured out what you meant by a 'dangerous dinner,' but this place hardly looks scary to me." As soon as Micheal braked, Carra had her hand on the door handle. She was starving. A two-story inn was attached to a charm of a restaurant with a long, sloping lawn and a sign that swung in the wind.

"It's *what* we're eating that's dangerous, not where—and neither are here. Close your eyes, put your feet up and don't ask questions, Carra. I'll be back in ten minutes."

He wasn't back for twenty, and when he returned he was trying to juggle two giant bags and a black, cast-iron frying pan. "What are you up to?" she demanded suspiciously.

"Making absolutely certain you're going to have a dinner you've never had before."

"Mike?"

"Hmm?"

"Fancy's wasted on me. I could eat sticks right now." She cast a last mournful glance at the inviting-looking restaurant, the view of which was fading all too fast from the rear window. So was the sun. In another hour it was going to be dark, and as far as she could tell they were headed even farther from home.

"You may want to eat sticks after you see what I've set up," he admitted. "We're talking a potential for failure that would give a Cordon Bleu chef ulcers."

She glanced at him. The trace of unsureness in his voice was unlike Mike. "Do you notice anyone in the car but you and me? No one's fussy in this crew."

"Promise?"

"With no problem at all," she assured him. It was twenty minutes before he pulled off the road onto a gravel path, and another five before the gravel path ended at a pond. The water was mirror-clear, shaped like a diamond and backdropped by century-old giant oaks and a grassy shore.

He climbed out of the car with a sigh of satisfaction for his picnic site, then glinted at her. "Are you in a nice, mystical, druidlike mood?"

"Heaven knows," she said, quickly becoming aware that they were having a camp-out dinner. "What does it take to be in a druidlike mood?"

"Just believing, Irish. Just letting it happen. It's easier than you know."

Her legs were tired, her stomach was cramped from hunger. It had really been an incredibly long day, and Mike was so full of nonsense. The sun kissed the treetops as he gathered firewood and arranged fifteen—exactly fifteen—stones in a circle for a firepit. "Logan stones. The druids fiercely believed in them, and you don't dare underestimate the power of Logan stones, not in Ireland. They're good for promises of longevity, a healthy future, and—" he paused expressively "—a hell of a sex life."

"Can we eat them?" she asked dryly.

"We are failing to get the *caillin's* mind off her stomach," he told the sunset, and proceeded to open and pour her a glass of dark ruby liquid from a good-sized bottle. The first sip told her it was sparkling grape, not wine.

"I seem to have given you good reason to doubt my capacity to hold any liquor," she teased him impishly.

"More relevant," he said firmly, "is that you don't need any spirits except for the ancient ones—and believe me, we're getting to those."

She was immune to spirits, but it was one of those nights when she couldn't be to Mike. He seemed to have found a place out of time—no people, no sounds, no civilized reminders of the real world. Her back rested against a fallen oak, her legs stretched out on a blanket. She listened to him ramble on about Irish legends and leprechauns.

He made far too big a fire. The red flames leaped and crackled and spit against a rapidly darkening sky. The woods behind them gradually turned ghost dark, huge and shadowed, and the smooth pond took on an ebony shine. She wondered how he'd ever found the place. She watched the fire turn his hair copper, his skin gold. It reflected off the dominantly strong lines of his face, and she wondered how long he'd been lonely.

A dangerous emotion swept through her, or perhaps not an emotion but simply a knowledge. That knowledge told her she didn't want Mike to have spent solitary hours discovering this enchanted place alone, building fires for no one, needing to talk and no one there to listen.

She pushed away the feeling. How crazy could a woman get? Mike tackled mountains for the love of the challenge, had the respect and caring of everyone she'd ever seen him with. He loved a crowd; heaven knew most women would love him, and the idea that he could need her was silly.

Almost as silly as Mike striding toward her and, serious as a judge, telling her, "If you stay within the firelight, the banshees can't get you. After dark you always have to worry about the banshees in Ireland. The fairies can't help you once the sun's down."

"Oh, really? What happens if I have a call of nature?"

"No problem. I lift all mystical incantations and spells for a call of nature." He reached down and grabbed a small branch. "I also outfit you with a shillelagh to ward off evil spirits."

"That stick's oak. I thought a true shillelagh had to be made out of blackthorn?"

"*My* shillelaghs do just fine as oak," he said reprovingly. "But if you *do* happen to need a quick stroll in the woods, I'd skip the shillelagh and head directly for the flashlight in the glove box. You're also going to be extremely careful to avoid poison ivy."

"Yes, sir."

He called after her, "And when you get back, sassy, all spells are on again."

By the time she'd rinsed her hands in the pond, he was serving dinner, one course at a time. The salad was a tossed blend of watercress and shamrocks, wooed to flavor with the tang of an invisibly flavored dressing and maybe the flourish with which it was served. "Shamrocks?" she said disbelievingly.

"They're an herb of the clover family. The white ones are inedible, but not the green. The Irish have valued the shamrock for luck over the centuries, but unless you eat them, there's no value. The symbol is for love, honor and wit, but only if you finish every bite on your plate."

"I am, I am." She was still chuckling when he produced the entrée: delicate fillets of bream, perch and tench, still sizzling from the fire.

"I'm not claiming these are good," he warned her. "Just that they're also Irish to the core. My goal was to produce a true Celtic dinner, and stereotypes of the old Irish stew just don't cut it. We're sea people, have always lived off the sea…and word has it that no one cooks fish worse than the Irish."

"You must be crazy. This is excellent. But you still haven't used that huge black frying pan."

"Ah, that."

For a moment her gaze locked on his face, certain she saw a flush climb his cheeks. Could Mike be embarrassed? He lurched to his feet the moment he was finished with the fish. "*What* is going into that frying pan?" she asked suspiciously.

"Dessert—and the dangerous part of the meal I promised you. Once you've tasted this particular dessert, I warn you, something mysterious will happen, something you can't explain, something which will leave nothing the same ever again."

"I want you to know, I'm shaking with worry."

"Skeptics are particularly susceptible."

She chuckled, but her curiosity was mounting like temperature from a flu. She set her plate on the blanket and wandered to his fire, all hot coals now with little flame. Over his shoulder, she watched him stir something in his black frying pan that looked strangely like a flower.

"It's an orchid. A uniquely Irish orchid, deliciously edible. Grown in the Dingle peninsula and known as the *meidhreach magairlín*."

"A beautiful name. But what does it mean?"

"I can't tell you." He stirred, added things from little containers he must have collected at the restaurant and stirred some more. Never once did he look at her face.

She couldn't take her eyes off his. "*Why* can't you tell me?"

"Because it's a crude name not fit for a lady."

She glared at the back of his neck. "Now you *have* to tell me. I can't stand it."

"If you'll look closely, maybe you'll figure it out and I won't have to."

She looked and saw nothing but a flower that looked similar to a delicate iris with two bulbs at its root, simmering in a sauce that was gradually tainting the air with a mysteriously sweet, tangy scent. His dessert "cooked" for almost fifteen minutes before he lifted the pan from the fire and spooned the mixture into two dishes.

"Now you taste . . . and you know you'll have taken the *Saspan Dubh*."

"That's the name of the spell?"

"Yes."

"So what's the name of the flower?"

"Cats are less curious than you are. Would you just try it?" He watched her test the first spoonful on her tongue. Her eyes widened with both surprise and delight, and he settled next to her as she finished the rest with wanton enthusiasm. "Already the spell is working. Total personality change," he observed. "No caution, no hesitation. Just fearless bravery and brazen courage in the face of the most dangerous risk."

"More relevant, is there a little more?"

"And greed. I've never seen the spell work this fast."

"There must be a spoonful more in that frying pan."

"The question is, where are you going to put it? I must have bought enough food for three men. There isn't a drop left."

"Is it my fault you turned out to be such a terrific chef?" His dinner had been delicious, but more than that she hadn't forgotten how worried he had seemed about the outcome. She stole the last spoonful, and then naturally carried the frying pan to the pond edge.

"I'll clean up," he insisted.

"Chefs cook. Riffraff clean up. That's just a fair division of labor, and that way you don't have to pretend you have the energy to move." It didn't take her long to sweep up their few dishes, rinse them and cart the bulk of their picnic debris to the car. By the time she headed back to the log, Mike was already there, head tipped back and legs stretched out. Replete and feeling lazy, she dropped down next to him. "Relaxed?"

"Close to catatonic."

"So tell me what your *meidhreach magairlín* means."

"Next year when you get old enough."

"I'm old enough. Trust me."

His gaze focused on her, his expression glinted with dry humor. "The common name for the *magairlín* orchid is merry testicles." He whispered the meaning in her ear.

She burst out laughing, not for the name but for the comical expression on his face.

"You laugh now, but the power of the *meidhreach magairlín* goes back centuries," he warned. "The ancient druids claimed there was no more powerful love spell than the orchid cooked in a black frying pan." He shrugged negligently. "Regrettably, there's no cure for the spell, no antidote, no hope of reversing its power. It's the most powerful magic in all of Ireland, and as we all know, that's saying a great deal."

"As we all know," Carra echoed teasingly, yet her laughter suddenly seemed to be suspended in the night. The last of the coals simmered like orange jewels; their pond had turned star-studded. There couldn't be magic, yet a murmur of yearning whispered through her, potent and real.

She wanted to be nowhere else but here, with him, for him. She wanted to be the woman he felt easy with, the woman he laughed with, the woman he trusted enough to show his vulnerable side. Mike was so damn strong. He was a man to make a woman believe in the romantic, the whimsical, the impossible.

Mike was dangerous magic, not because of his Logan stones and *meidhreach magairlín* and love spells, but because of the capacity for tenderness in his eyes.

Those eyes suddenly came much closer. For so long she'd convinced herself her defensive instincts were as strong as stone. She didn't feel much like stone when his lips brushed her forehead, her cheek and then her mouth.

His palm found the bare, white skin of her throat, and a crisp night abruptly turned sultry. His lips first tested, then tasted, then rubbed. The scrape of flint on flint caused sparks. This was that kind of friction, only softer, drowning soft, midnight soft.

His lean, long body was already next to hers. She clutched his shoulders when he eased her away from the log, down to the rough, wool blanket. His mouth never lessened its velvet assault, and then her senses were barraged, distracted, lured away from what his lips were doing.

His skin smelled like heat. A woman could get lost, covered by those shoulders. His hard thighs and lazy, slow hands—those hands discovered bare skin beneath her sweater. She discovered that intimacy could be a taste. A sound. A fierce, sweet, blindingly delicious need.

You lied to me, Mike. All the days and hours of working together. Her trusting that he'd been content with the friendship she'd so carefully worked at building.

His lips, his body, his hands told her other truths. He wanted her. He'd never stopped wanting her. She heard the rush of wind in the night, smelled grass and water, watched her own hands slide into his hair in a wash of defenselessness.

His hunger was so honest, so real. Other times, his kisses had shown patience, sensitivity, a lover's skills. Now he'd forgotten his lover's skills. He was too busy tearing her apart with the lushness of passion and promise, the lure of being taken and cherished, the magic of a spinning, black sky and Mike's bold, dark eyes.

She tore away, breathing so hard her lungs rasped in oxygen. It took her a moment to move. Her limbs had no more energy, and her heart was beating like a freight train. If he had pursued . . . but he didn't pursue. When she pushed up against the log, he simply coiled to a sitting position and looked at her.

"You changed the rules," she accused him. Her breath was still frantic.

"I never made any rules where you were concerned."

"I told you from the very beginning—"

"I know what you told me."

"I thought you understood—"

"I understand exactly what happens every time I touch you, every time you touch me. You turn to fire, and I burn up." The hint of humor in his voice died. His tone turned into a whisper, layers of silver, layers of steel. "We're going to be lovers, Carra."

Her tongue was suddenly desert dry. A dangerously strong yearning clutched inside of her. Images flew through her mind, images of lying under Mike, bare, helpless, skin coated with passion and the heat of wanting, the heat of being needed.

Her whole body tensed. She sprang up and away from him and jammed trembling fingers in the pockets of her skirt. "No."

He never budged from his relaxed position. His elbow still rested on his bent knee, and his low voice never rose above a whisper. "I want a name for the bastard, Irish. I'm more than willing to fight your ghost for you, but I need a clue, a name, some idea what I'm up against."

A chill streaked down her spine. Magic died with the sharpness of a knife blade.

"You're still holding a torch for the baby's father? Or is it that he dragged you from here to hell and you're holding it against all men?"

"What is this, multiple guess? *Neither* of the above, Micheal. Leave me alone!"

He got up, looked at her, then reached for the blanket. As soon as it was stuffed in the car, he drove her home. She wasn't used to Mike in a silence, Mike without an easy grin, Mike without lazy, easy conversation. He wasn't brooding, just quiet, and the drive was interminably long.

When they finally arrived at the cottages, it was past midnight. Neither had left lights on, and fog swirled around the car where he parked. She felt as if her brain was a fog, too, thick and dark, nothing she could push away, nothing she could help. She reached for the door handle, desperate to get away, when Mike captured her wrist.

"Carra, I'm thirty-four. If you're afraid I'm playing some kind of game with you, don't be. I'm not a complicated man, and there's nothing as easy as honesty. I'm tired of climbing the mountains alone, and I know exactly what I want and need in my life. A woman with the courage to outlast the ups and downs, a woman I can laugh and talk and fight with, a lover who's as demanding as I am."

"And I've been trying to tell you—"

"That you don't feel any of those things? Who are you trying to fool, you or me? The air sizzles every time you and I are in the same room. Your pulse slams every time I kiss you, and mine shoots from here to hell. You're sassy and you're proud and you're funny and you're beautiful. And you're too damn smart to let one round with a bastard ruin your life."

He released her wrist and reached over her to open her door. "Get over him, Irish. Damn fast. You're no coward, and I'm fast running out of patience with cold showers."

She closed the door as quietly as any lady, and then threw off her jacket and kicked her shoes halfway across the room. The nerve of him! The arrogance, the egotism. Who could have guessed he was capable of that kind of cruelty?

She lit a lamp, shed clothes, threw on a nightgown and started pacing. Mike had a lot in common with a railroad. Just plow down those tracks without any sensitivity for anything in his path. Push, push, push. Now that she thought about it, he'd been pushing her since she met him. He'd pushed her into that horrible meeting in the bar with the work crew. He'd pushed her into that wretched confrontation with Mc-Illenney. Now he thought he could push her into an affair by implying she was a coward. Who the devil ever said she wanted the man?

The cottage was freezing. She lit a fire, fixed the grate and curled up on the hearth, knees bent, arms wrapped around them.

She ached all over from wanting him. The symptoms were rather like flu: headache, stomach churning, palms damp, heart pounding. She pushed at her temples, miserable.

Nothing was going well. A normal man would never have been this difficult to handle. Normal men didn't cook flowers, didn't take a woman to neck on a rath, didn't talk about little people and banshees. She hadn't forgotten the wisp of a kiss stolen at the top of Blarney Castle, either.

When Mike was being a hardheaded, stubborn Pict, he was difficult enough to handle. When he was being romantic, he pushed at defenses Carra had spent two long years building up. He didn't play fair. He was also blind. He'd said what he wanted—a strong, assertive, mountain climber of a lover.

She wasn't that. She was just an ordinary woman. A scared woman—lots scared, honest scared, soul scared. In the past her judgment about men had been worth horseradish. Falling in love was fun. Falling off a cliff was probably fun, too, until you hit rock bottom.

Two years ago she'd been at rock bottom. And she couldn't risk hurting someone else while she came to terms with her mistakes.

But for Mike to accuse her of cowardice—that was low.

Mike jerked off his jacket, shoved off his shoes and paced. He shouldn't have pushed her, not that hard, not that fast.

He pulled off his shirt, threw it, dragged a hand through his hair, paced. He hadn't touched her, had he? If he had no sense of honor, he'd have crushed that soft mouth and taken her. They had something; he could have proved it then. Instead, he'd tried talking to her. Obviously that was a stupid mistake.

He pulled open cupboard doors, searching for something. Whiskey? There was a half-filled bottle of cognac that Gallagher had brought him on a Friday night. He slammed the cupboard closed before he remembered to pour it. He paced some more.

He hadn't had a decent night's sleep since she got here. And for what? For an illusion that she could matter to him more than heaven or hell, for an instinct that she needed him, for an impulse that she could be a man's rock, that he would never find a lover quite like her. What a crock. She'd told him she didn't want a relationship. Why couldn't he get it through his thick skull that she simply didn't want him?

The cabin was broiling. He threw open a window. Not surprising him at all, the thick, fleecy fog had turned into rain.

Surprising him totally was the knock on the door.

Shocking him more was Carra throwing it open, hands on hips and those soft blue eyes blazing. "How *dare* you accuse me of a lack of courage, Fitzgerald!"

Rage and frustration diminished in him faster than fire could warm. There were tears in her eyes. He stood stock-still on the far side of the room.

"I've got news for you, Mike. If and when I want a man, I'll have the courage to tell him. If and when I want a lover, I'll take a lover. I make my own choices, take my own risks, pay my own piper. I also say no if I want to say no, because that's my choice, not because I'm carrying around a lot of past emotional baggage."

"Okay, Carra." Softly, quietly, he moved forward to close the door. She hadn't moved from where she was rigidly standing.

"Implying I was carrying a torch for another man was damn dirty pool on your part. Cats will fly before I forgive you that one."

"I don't blame you. I was way out of line."

"You have a lot of things confused."

"Yes."

He let her tell him all those things he had confused. He didn't want to hear it all. He wanted to hold her.

The man's name had been Aaron. He was a commercial pilot with crazy work hours, and they'd known each other for two years before the relationship actually became an affair. She'd loved him—without reserve, without sense—and had every reason to believe he loved her. They'd talked rings and futures and children.

"He wanted children and so did I. That's why I never really worried when I discovered I was pregnant. Neither of us were careless—God, how can anyone be careless about a child?—but I couldn't take the pill. So we used a less effective method that failed. It was as simple as that. I hadn't told him yet. I was supposed to see him on Thursday..." All Carra could see was Mike's face through a blur. "But the Tuesday before that I had a visitor. Actually four visitors. A woman and three children. Three children, Mike! One of her babies was too small to walk."

When her voice broke, his heart did. Her eyes were blind with thick, unshed tears. "Sweetheart, don't do this to yourself," he said helplessly, but stopping her flood of words was like willing her to cry. She couldn't.

"I had *no* idea. None. Talk about blind and stupid. His wife lived three miles away from me! I dropped him like a hot potato. Good Lord, do you think I'm the kind of woman who would break up a home and family? You think I still cared about him?"

"I think you cared like hell." The closest chair was a horsehair relic. He eased down and pulled her with him. She was shell-shock rigid, and she might not have wanted his arms around her. He needed his arms around her.

"I didn't care a whit!"

"Okay, you didn't care a whit." He smoothed her hair.

"But I cared about the baby. I wanted that baby, but I was so upset the day that woman visited me. When she was gone I left the house and started walking. It was raining and cold, and I didn't think. I was responsible for that baby, Mike, and I didn't think! By the time I got home, I was already sick."

"Dammit, Irish. You haven't talked yourself into believing losing the baby was your fault?" He kissed the top of her forehead, wrapped her up, warmed her and snuggled her and held her.

"It was my fault, and that's when it all started to pile up. I kept thinking . . . what kind of judgment did I have? As a woman, as a mother? To pick that kind of man to father her? I was old enough. I was twenty-three when I met him; that's plenty old enough. If I hadn't been so busy being *romanced*, maybe I could have opened my eyes to some honest reality. There had to have been clues he was married. I just never looked for them. And when a woman's done that good a job of proving to herself that she has rotten judgment—"

"Honey, he was the bastard. Not you."

"I was the idiot. Not him."

"Shh." He nuzzled his chin to the top of her head and just waited. The emotional explosion was over; he didn't even want to think about how long she'd been holding it in. A lit fuse of dynamite always blew, but then it was done. The letdown had to happen. Adrenaline only pumped so long. Hearts didn't understand about a rage of hurt; they wanted to tick-tick-tick like everything was all right again.

Everything was all right again. He intended to be around to make sure of that. Now, tomorrow, next year and a hundred years from now. Knights and heroes would undoubtedly be reacting better to her story than he was. Caveman mentality, regrettably, seemed to suit him better. No man but him was getting anywhere near Carra again. The right to love, hold, comfort—even the right to hurt—he took those rights. As of now.

He heard her sigh, limp and exhausted. He held her tighter, thinking she had fallen asleep. He thought of the limitless, uncomfortable possibilities of spending the night cramped in a horsehair-stuffed chair built for midgets. He thought of how exactly right she fit in his arms, how perfectly her head fit in his shoulder, how rich and rare the feelings of protectiveness and loving swamped him.

"I need you to believe me, Mike," she said softly.

"Believe you?"

"It bothered me, badly, when you asked me if I was one of those women who hold it against all men because one hurt them." Her head jerked up, and he saw a sadness and a pride in her eyes that made his heart ache. "It was never like that. I never had you confused with Aaron; I never thought you were like him. I want you to believe that."

"All right," he murmured.

"Maybe caution's been my ghost. Caution pokes up when anyone's afraid of getting hurt again, but it's also a natural result of facing up to mistakes a person's made. I know exactly what mistakes I made— believing in candlelight and romance and moonlight, believing in roses. It wasn't Aaron or any other man that knocked those illusions out of me. It was life.''

He waited. She was fumbling for words, grasping for pride, honesty and something else he couldn't fathom.

''I can't—won't—make those mistakes again, but that's not to say I have no feelings, no wants, no needs,'' she said slowly. ''I already told you just how it was. If I wanted an affair with a man, I would be honest with him. If I wanted a lover, I would have the courage to take that lover.''

Silence fell, while Mike found cotton wool forming in his throat, making it difficult to swallow, making it difficult for him to talk. Slowly, with infinite caution and care, he brushed back the hair from her cheek.

''*Are* you considering taking a lover, Carra O'Neill?''

Seven

The twenty men in front of Carra were stretched out everywhere from the window seats to the stone benches in the Great Hall. Arrows and crossbows lay on the table behind her, so did examples of four-teenth-century armored chest plates and headgear.

Her assembled tourist crew was a good bunch, and the group of men as receptive and interested as the women had been this morning. Her lecture was nearly through, and it was one of her favorite subjects.

"You'll never be able to play the role of knight unless you know what defending a castle really meant," she told the group. "Fire, poisoning the water and tunneling were the most common methods of enemy attack. Glencorrah is equipped to defend against those methods. Our moat, for example, isn't out there just to make a pretty pond. The purpose of a moat was to make it impossible for the enemy to tunnel under a castle's foundation.''

She sensed the instant Mike appeared in the north archway. She knew it because her temperature rose ten degrees, her breasts suffered instant arousal, and her pulse started rattling.

He didn't enter, and he only stayed long enough to level her a wink and let his eyes dawdle over the fit of her red blouse and gray jeans. An ardent lover might deliver such a thorough inspection, and his gaze promised passionate interest. His grin was wicked . . . and intimate. When he disappeared from sight, he took all of her concentration with him.

Two weeks, nearly three, had passed since the night he'd asked her if she were considering taking a lover. Her answer had been yes.

Since then she'd rather unexpectedly been living the life of a nun. It wasn't that they weren't spending hours together every day, but Mike seemed terribly confused. ''Yes'' did not mean that she'd suddenly locked herself in a fourteenth-century chastity belt. The last she knew, yes meant yes.

''When the tourists walk through our doors on the first of August, they're going to find a castle in the middle of a siege,'' Carra managed to continue to the group. ''A siege was the most interesting method of attack in medieval times, because it involved the element of bluff. Basically a well-built castle could hold out as long as the will to resist remained, so the enemy had to count on demoralizing the castle forces. Our imaginary enemy is going to try to bluff us into believing his supplies will outlast ours, worry us into thinking he's stronger and better prepared to with-stand a long siege than we are. In short, bluff was the name of the game.''

Within a half hour she finished her talk, invited questions, and then suggested the men come up and try on the armor and get the feel of holding the cross-bows. A warmer, friendlier group would be hard to find, but none of them made her heart swing, her pulse unravel, her nerves clutch.

Only Mike, the man who was slowly but surely driving her crazy, did that. They seemed to be playing a game of bluff, only what was there to bluff? She wanted him for a lover and had said so. She'd asked nothing from him. The opposite was true. She had never once hinted that she wanted a commitment or a future beyond their weeks together.

Sunlight glinted on a shield of armor that one of the tourist crew picked up. The shield was thick, heavy metal. A lance wouldn't dent it, neither would ar-rows. A month before, she'd come to Glencorrah to be just like that armor, just like the fortress of the keep: invincible, strong, invulnerable.

Her world hadn't totally changed colors. She wasn't yet sure of herself. Trust in her own judgment still troubled her. She hadn't razed all her old enemies, but she had found something stronger than her resis-tance.

Mike forgot to eat if he wasn't coaxed, so she did the coaxing. She could sneak a laugh out of him even when he was exhausted and he needed someone to talk to during his bouts of insomnia. She wasn't going to go so raving out of her tree as to label her emotions love, but the darn man! It wasn't his feeding those wicked orchids to her that made her feel this way, but the way he listened to her, believed in her, was a man so pricelessly worth loving.

Never mind the labels. Never mind if she'd just invited life to kick her in the teeth again, and never mind if she didn't believe in happily-ever-afters. She believed in Mike.

She'd said yes. She'd meant yes.

So what was the bullheaded Pict waiting for?

"Carra?"

As the last of the men cleared out, she saw Sean striding toward her, grime from head to toe and his hard hat pushed back at a cocky angle. As honorary guardian angels went, hers lacked a halo. The macho nonsense was all show. McIllenney was a born and bred fussbudget, and she rued the day she ever made friends with him. He fussed over her worse than a mother.

"How did the meeting with your lads go?" he demanded briskly. "Ran over a little late, didn't it?"

"Maybe a half hour."

"Thought I'd help you chase them out of here, but I can see you've done that. Running it a little close, weren't you? It's nearly five o'clock. You got any other irons in the fire, I'll take the ball. Feel free to scram, pronto."

"Am I missing something here?" she asked wryly. "Scramming, pronto, wasn't on my agenda. I've got a pile of applications to look through for the head of my tourist staff. And after that—"

His frown was impatient. "You're running peace-maker for Killimer and Fitzgerald, aren't you? I thought he said the dinner was at six, then back here for a run through the castle by seven-thirty." He scratched his chin, eyeing her with sudden uneasiness. "You're not going to the dinner?"

Her eyes were frankly bewildered. "I don't know what dinner you're talking about. And what's this about 'running peacemaker'?"

"Nothing. Could be I got a real big mouth," Sean said to the vaulted ceiling, and then sighed. "Well now." He sighed again. "Glad your meeting went real nice, but any of the local lads give you trouble now, you just send 'em to me. I told you—"

"I know what you told me." Three weeks ago she wouldn't have dreamed of draping an arm around McIllenney's shoulders, but every day a little of Fitzgerald's gutsy nerve was rubbing off on her. "Now you're going to tell me what could possibly be wrong between our nice Mr. Killimer and our imminently sweet Mr. Fitzgerald."

"Who said anything was wrong?"

"Tomorrow I thought I'd try one of your earth movers. Did I tell you about the summer job I had—"

"O'Neill, you have no honor, no respect, no mercy. If you'd been raised in this country like a good Irish woman—"

"Mike goes up to Limerick every week. I thought they got on fine."

"Fine?" McIllenney snorted. "Mother Macrae, lass—"

"Skip the Mother Macraes and let's hear it."

At seven-thirty that evening, strictly by accident, Carra was pacing around the gatehouse. Also by accident, she was wearing a black-and-white checked skirt, black silk blouse and killer heels. Her war paint started with mascara, applied with a mercilessly light hand. Other weapons included a dose of perfume, a dangle of ebony from her ears and wrist, a lucky charm only God could see and a handmade Irish shawl.

The evening was fresh and cool, the castle grounds hushed. The sun hovered over the west parapet like a soft, yellow ball, and her heart was beating like a sledgehammer. She hadn't exactly been invited to this shindig. Mike just might be a bit irritated to find his party crashed.

A glossy black Rolls covered the hill around 7:35. By the time it parked, Carra had her most diplomatic smile plastered in place and was moving toward the car. Mike climbed out of the far side.

She only had eyes for Mr. Killimer, who, chauffeur-assisted, climbed out from the side closest to her. Starting with a gold-tipped ebony cane, he was five feet four inches of spruced-up bantam rooster. His kelly-green jacket boasted an ascot, jauntily sprinkled with shamrocks; he wore white shoes and an ostentatious pin—a coat of arms—on his lapel. The first time she'd met him, she'd suspected his white mane had a little color assist, and his pale blue eyes were snob's eyes—cool, judgmental, unforgiving.

He'd interviewed and hired her in Boston, over a long dinner that had gone very well. The trick to getting along with Mr. Killimer was simply understanding that he was slightly impressed with himself. He liked people to know he had lots of money, and he liked people to kowtow. Carra hadn't minded a little kowtowing.

Mike would. In the two hours since she'd talked with Sean, that was all she could think about. Mike was big, strong, whip-smart, sexy, funny and occasionally arrogant. But he was always going to be a total failure as a kowtower.

Added to that, she had no idea Mike had been taking on the crew's battles with Mr. Killimer from the first day of the project. Possibly the reason her heart was thumping like a sledgehammer was because someone should have hit her with one. If she had any sensitivity, she would have known. He never mentioned his weekly meetings with Killimer. She knew both men and could have guessed they'd relate like chalk and cheese. Mike was everyone's bolster, catalyst and buoy, but he was too bullheaded and proud to hint he had troubles of his own.

Carra could hardly sit in the cottage and worry that he needed help when she wasn't there. She surged forward the moment Mr. Killimer noticed her and planted a European kiss on both his wintered cheeks.

He was surprised to see her, but not unwelcoming. His cheeks had a scarlet flush; there was a certain tightness in his face. Anger. Control. A gentleman didn't display such emotions, and he had never been less than a gentleman around her. He was glad to have the chance to see her. She hoped he'd had a good dinner. While that kind of idiotic patter went on she had the chance to take stock of his six-foot-three-inch sidekick.

Mike looked dauntingly magnificent in white linen and tie. He also looked dauntingly furious the moment he caught sight of her. She was inclined to remind him that he never took his temper out on a woman, but that wasn't an easy thing to slip into the conversation. His feelings for gate-crashers were clear though, because his mouth was a white line, his stride had a soldier's rigidity, and his expression was reminiscent of a caged lion about to snap through his bars.

So dinner had been the pits.

Woman or not, she saddled her imaginary white steed and laced on her armor. Blithe and happy, she laced an arm through Mr. Killimer's and squeezed affectionately, blocking off the X-ray glare Mike was trying to shoot her. "I'm so glad to have the chance to see you again! Talking on the phone isn't the same thing at all as seeing you in person. Is your leg still giving you trouble?"

"Constant grief, lass, constant grief. Without my cane I don't know how I'd get around."

"And here it's such a long walk to tour around the castle. You don't mind if I join you, do you? I know you wanted to talk nuts and bolts with Mike, but I'll be quiet as a mouse, I promise."

Truthfully she'd never talked more. From the stables to the keep, from the solar to the dungeons, she chatted up Mr. Killimer—his health, his family, his horses, his endless charitable hobbies. She assured him that Glencorrah would be appreciated for centuries to come because of him. She let him lean on her until her arm and leg ached. She listened to a long dissertation on disrespectful help and the arrogance of the lower classes. She smiled, and she felt Mike's eyes boring into her back from room to room, parapet to battlement.

Mr. Fitzgerald rather reminded her of water boiling under a closed pot close to explosion. He was terse bordering on rude. He presented facts like bullets and figures like weapons. He really wasn't behaving at all well.

Mike wasn't handleable; Mr. Killimer was. The old gent blossomed for flattery, flushed for her smiles and rambled on and on about ancient Irish history when coaxed. Mr. Killimer was a perfect gentleman once he cooled down.

By the time the chauffeur-driven Rolls was gliding away, a sunset rainbowed the hills. Carra didn't really notice. She was tired and drained from tension, and her feet were killing her. She really didn't have the energy left to face the giant Pict with the totem-pole stone face, but she didn't have many other options.

Behind Mike the castle rose rock-strong, fortress-powerful. The castle had nothing on his expression. His tie flapped in the night wind, and his shoulders were braced like a block of ice. There was something raw in his eyes, a blaze of some emotion she had no name for and had never seen before.

Her skirt whipped around her legs; she pushed at it. She tried cheerfulness. "Glad that's over?"

"What the devil did you think you were doing?"

He probably thought she was intimidated because her heart was thundering. "Aren't you going to tell me what happened at dinner?"

"Sure, I'll tell you what happened at dinner. Killimer got it in his head that we could open Glencorrah a few weeks early if I instituted a few shortcuts. Now it's your turn. How did you even know this dinner and tour were planned?"

"What shortcuts?" she demanded stubbornly.

"He wanted me to cheat on the specs, cut the quality of materials we'd been using and lengthen the crew's workday to sixteen hours."

"I'm sure you told him no, politely."

"I told him to shove it, and he's lucky I didn't strangle him as well." There was no rage in his voice. If anything his tenor was cold and distracted, but there was that look in his eyes again as he focused on her. That raw look of emotions on the edge. "As you could see, he was alive and well. I didn't strangle him over dinner, and we came to terms. My terms. Battles don't frighten me, Carra. I thought you knew that."

"I knew *that*," she agreed. "I didn't know that my showing up was going to bother you this much."

"Your joining the twosome didn't bother me at all. Killimer always intended to stop in and see you. You haven't had anything but phone contact since you got here. But that isn't why you showed up."

"Not exactly."

"Try telling me, exactly, why you came."

She hesitated. "It occurred to me that you might have an occasional tiny problem with personalities and Mr. Killimer. I thought there was some small chance you might run into an awkward situation. I thought it might help to have an extra person on hand to diffuse that. I thought—"

"Think? Give us another, Irish. You barely gave me a chance to get in two words with Killimer. As far as I could tell, you were headlong, headstrong determined to take a bullet for me."

"You could have needed help," she said stubbornly.

"You think I'd use a woman if I did? You think I'd use you?"

Cripes, he was being difficult. She walked the bear home and let the moonlight soothe him. The big oaf seemed to lose his testy moodiness over the half-hour walk to the cottages, but she expected he'd pace to the wee hours if she let him go home alone.

Mike had insomnia if the wind blew wrong. Tonight there was no problem with wind, but with her. She knew she'd interfered, which was a federal crime. Just possibly she'd been slightly out of line, but she wasn't about to take a lot of nonsense just because she'd dared to step in and help him for a change.

Just like a dozen other nights, she pushed at the knob when they reached her door. "I'll brew some coffee."

"Thanks, no, not this late."

"Then I'll get you a shot of whiskey. Don't give me a hard time, Mike. You're coming in, and you're going to relax."

He came in and went so far as to close the door. She paid no attention, simply moved around him as if she wasn't dealing with a bit of volatile nitroglycerine. The fire needed a peat brick; her shawl had to be folded and put away. She shed her shoes, switched on a lamp, and then disappeared into the small kitchen area to pour him a shot of whiskey.

When she returned she found him leaning against the rough chimney wall by the fireplace. He was about as relaxed as the fire poker. Every time their eyes met, she saw something in his that tried to swallow her, body, heart, soul. He didn't touch the whiskey.

She didn't have a prayer of sitting still, so didn't try. She unclipped her earrings, drew off the bracelet, absently straightened things and talked. Construction was nearly done. They were on the last few projects now, could he believe it? She was interviewing a woman named Moira O'Brien tomorrow. "If she's as good as her qualifications—and with Mr. Killimer's approval, of course—she'll be the permanent head of staff once I'm gone. Rather funny feeling, hiring your own replacement. She doesn't have a background in 'living museums,' so the sooner I get her on board—"

"Stop it, Carra."

Her head whipped in his direction, and something stilled inside her. He hadn't moved. The soft lamplight blurred and muted the whole room with a glow, but the glow didn't seem to work on Mike. His features were harsh, shadowed and tense, his eyes dangerously brooding.

"Stop what?"

"Is that what you want to do? Fluff pillows? Talk shop?"

All the breath wanted to lodge in her lungs. A nestling, warm cottage had suddenly turned cool, and a man capable of immense gentleness was suddenly not.

"I didn't realize fluffing pillows was a capital offense," she said wryly.

"It isn't, if that's what you want to do."

"I don't know what you mean."

"I've been watching you take the miles every day. And you walked a damn long mile tonight, just to take a bullet you thought was aimed in my direction. Now come another mile."

When a man was being that obscure, a woman could certainly get away with pretending she didn't know what he meant. Unfortunately, Carra did know. She stood absolutely still for a moment, and then moved forward. His eyes waited when she touched his cheek, raised up on tiptoe and placed her mouth over his.

It was meant as a gentling kiss, and he responded not at all. The devil didn't want to be gentled. He wanted trouble. His eyes dared her to give him trouble.

Her pulse eclipsed all known speed records, and her palms turned damp. She didn't believe in knights and fairy tales, but there had been times that made her believe: when Mike had kissed her, when she'd felt swept off her feet and lured into forgetting time and place and good common sense. Mike was no knight, no duke, no dragon fighter. He'd pushed her from the day she met him, pushed her into doing things she couldn't do, wasn't ready for, couldn't handle. He deserved a good shaking.

He was too big to shake. Unsure and a little angry, she withdrew her mouth from his and stood there, listening to his breathing, avoiding his eyes, staring at his mouth. She felt raw and untried. She felt confusion and inadequacy building like a tidal wave. And then she said a mental to-hell-with-Mike's-mood and took his mouth a second time.

She wanted this. She'd wanted it for weeks. It wasn't as if she wanted the whole darn world; she only desired a corner of it—the corner where his cool, smooth lips crushed under hers and her senses jangled and sang for the taste of him. Mike, tomb-still, did nothing when her arms slid around his neck.

It wasn't nice, kissing a tomb. It was awkward, and she felt more awkward yet when she moved in closer, rubbing closer, where silk wooed starched linen and her skirt swirled around his thighs. She wasn't sure when she stopped feeling awkward. It seemed to be when she stopped caring whether she was capable of seducing him.

If Mike wanted an adept lover, he was out of luck. If he was looking for more trouble than he could handle, though, she volunteered. He was welcome to stand there like a rock; his mouth was still under her dominion. She claimed tastes, textures, the shape of his lips, teased his tongue out of hiding and ravished it.

His neck had to be chafing under starched collar and tie. She tugged at the tie and fumbled with the button, aware that her fingers were less than steady, less than skilled, but not caring.

She closed her eyes, let kisses simmer on his lips and chin and throat and felt her calf muscles start to quake from standing too long on tiptoe. He was too tall, a common genetic problem of the pagan Picts. That height combined with his breadth, though, made for a wealth of playground material that other men simply didn't have.

Her fingers skimmed, clutched, rolled over his muscled shoulders, tiptoed over his chest, splayed on his ribs and then slid possessively around his back. She took his mouth again and again, forgetting politeness, forgetting shyness and modesty. Forgetting that she just didn't do this with a man. Any man.

The tomb was finally yielding. His body heat, the rasp of his breath, his heart leaping under her hand all told her. The only problem was her. Her legs wanted to pleat like an accordion. Her fingers were increasingly unsteady. Her breasts, swollen beneath her blouse, were hurting her. A lot of things were suddenly hurting. Her fingertips. Her hair. Her heart.

She broke off the last kiss and caught a glimpse of the glow in his eyes. But it was his hint of a smile that undid her.

"This is what you wanted all this time," she whispered helplessly. "For me to come to you?"

"For you to come to me." So simple.

"You're not angry with me about crashing the tour?" she tested.

"Yes." But the warrior's harshness was gone. "If you were seven years old, I'd take you over my knee. Killimer's a bigot and a snob, and we clash, I admit it. But the day I expect anyone else to take on my battles is a day that isn't going to happen. Don't do it again, Irish."

"A man can be proud to a fault," she mentioned.

"And a woman can occasionally forget everything she's afraid of—when she feels something stronger than fear. You made a dangerous mistake tonight by showing me how much you cared."

"Two weeks ago I offered—"

"Two weeks ago you were still defending your castle." Her silk blouse buttoned at the back. His lips whispered in her hair as he undid them. "Two weeks ago you thought you could go to bed with a man and not call it love, not really be touched on the inside, not risk anything too close to the heart."

"Mike . . ." Her blouse was gone, her skirt shivering down her hips, and all she could do was look in his eyes.

"Don't waste any time thinking you're safe, Carra. You're not safe, not with me. I want it all, everything you have, everything you are, no hiding and no holding back." Lord, why was he talking? He'd been *talking* to her for weeks.

With a rough sound, he bent his head and took her mouth as he'd wanted to take it all along. He'd wanted to see her bare from the day he met her, and except for the scrap of lace hugging her hips, he had her bare.

Her breasts were firm and small, the nipples as hard as brown beads when he slid a palm over them. He kneaded and rubbed her tiny nipples until she made a hoarse sound from deep in her throat and her fingers suddenly clutched in his hair.

His mouth raked across hers, then crushed so hard and possessively that her neck arched and her eyes closed and a fierce shudder took her body. Her fingers pushed at his shirt buttons. She was too slow. He pushed her hands away, fumbled at the buttons himself. He was too slow; her fingers pushed his away.

He almost laughed, and he thought of all the times he wanted to laugh in bed with Carra, but it wasn't time for that now. It had taken forever to win her trust. She'd fought real caring, because she was so damn sure life was going to hand her another blow. She was strong and good and whole and beautiful, and she could take it. But Carra believing that couldn't come from him.

Loving was all that could come from him now. And she'd take it before she had the chance to think, worry and build up all those outstanding defenses of hers again.

One of his shirt buttons pinged in the fire, startling her. In another moment his shirt was flying across the room. His chest was big and bare and gold, his eyes no more than a slash of green fire as he drew her down. "Touch me, honey. I want to feel your hands. I need you to feel what you do to me."

He moved her hands to his belt buckle; she felt the quake of impossible inadequacy tremble through her. She didn't have the kind of courage, not to be an aggressive lover. His face looked harsh, and the intensity in his eyes was pagan, raw, male. She thought of an unleashed falcon. She thought of all those knights that she didn't believe in, knights who would woo until a woman's senses were blind and she didn't have to think, knights who have the courtesy and chivalry to make the first time easy on a lady.

Mike had no intention of making it easy. He didn't want warmth; he wanted fire. He didn't want a woman to ease a physical need; he wanted to consume, take over, possess, shatter. And from the feel of his urgency, he had no patience left.

Touching him was like lighting a dynamite fuse. His skin turned into liquid heat, and his muscles tensed with rolling impatience. She undid the buckle, the zipper, and when he shook off the rest of his clothes

she skimmed her hands on his firelit chest, brazenly
stroked his hip and let her fingers coil around his
hardness. Maybe she found courage because he'd fed
her those wicked orchids.

Maybe she was simply coming apart at the seams.
Stretched out full against him, she wanted to. He was
crushably huge, and she'd never felt smaller. Her
breasts ached, rubbing against him, teased by the graze
of his rough chest hair. When his big hands slid her
silk panties down, she felt a wave of heat wash over
her. He knew things to do with his hands that he
shouldn't know, did things he shouldn't do. She told
him not to. She told him . . .

"You haven't even started to hurt yet, love," he
whispered. "You're not even halfway to where I want
you. Making love is only good when two people are
naked on the inside. More, Carra. More, honey, I
want more."

He wanted too much. She felt exposed in a way that
had nothing to do with bare skin, vulnerable as she'd
never felt vulnerable as a woman. Mike was rash,
reckless. A woman could burn up this way; the ache
inside could tear her in two. He didn't care. He
stroked, deep inside of her, until a soft, raw whisper
broke in her throat. He used his tongue and teeth and
lips on her breasts, until they were tight and hard, until they were swollen with yearning.

She wrapped her legs around him, softly, softly,
trying to defuse the wild speed, the unbearably building tension. He wouldn't listen. Where her touch was
gentle, he covered her hands, guiding them where he
wanted them, teaching her to stroke in a bolder way,
a more nakedly sexual way . . . a more honest way. His

body was hers. He expected her to claim it, take it, use it.

She didn't know honesty in lovemaking, not that way. She no longer knew a lot of things. The hearth was cold and hard. She didn't notice. A draft seeped under the door and contrasted to the blanketing heat of the fire. She noticed neither. At some point a belt buckle pressed into her spine, and her toe sent something clattering. There was a bed right in the next room. She didn't care.

"Look at me, Carra," he whispered. "Look at me now, and don't look away."

Through a blurred mist, she saw his eyes, when he finally moved over her. He wound her legs around him, and she felt a slow burning push when he entered her body, and his eyes never left hers. He withdrew and advanced until she could accommodate all of him, until a moan escaped her lips, a moan of abandon, a moan of longing. Feeling impaled was a delicious, wicked sensation. It wasn't enough. She wanted him to touch clear to her womb; she wanted a hard, fast rhythm and she wanted it now. Dammit, he knew. His deep dark eyes reflected back everything she wanted, everything she felt.

She reached up, claimed his mouth like a woman in heat, a woman in love, a woman who didn't give a hoot in hell if the sky fell. "Love me," she said fiercely, not a whisper but a demand, not a lady's voice but a wanton's. "Dammit, love me, Mike. Please. Please...please."

He gave her what she wanted, maybe not what he did. The touch of her hands, the look in her eyes, the intimate feel of her sheathed him, tight, wet, hot. He wanted it to last forever. He wanted her like this forever, undone and unraveled, eyes darker than midnight, wild with passion and in a fury of need and so damned beautiful.

Cascading shudders pulsed through her, undoing the last of his control. An earthquake of need exploded; he was helpless to stop it, had the insane feeling that he was burning alive with pleasure. He was burning, but he took Carra with him.

Eight

———

Rain had started pelting the windows around two in the morning. Irish rain had nothing in common with Boston rain. Boston rain was gray and dreary. Irish rain painted the land with a fresh coat of green, coated the windows with crystals and diamonds and made a woman think of fantasies.

Mike, lying next to her, looked extraordinarily real. His boxy chin was softened in the dark. His hair was all disheveled. He was naked and warm, took up all the space in the bed and even asleep kept an arm draped across her.

Real lovers, though, didn't really make love the way Mike had made love with her. Want couldn't really tear a person in two; pleasure really couldn't be earth-shattering. Making love with a man shouldn't have the power to take everything she was sure of and believed in and shake those values like a rag pillow.

Carra, wide awake as an owl, couldn't stop looking at him. She'd wanted to make love with him. She'd willingly given him part of herself, but not to the inclusion of all reality. She'd loved once with no sense and no judgment. She'd sworn to never let her heart rule her head again.

Reality was knowing that Glencorrah was nearly completed. Reality was knowing she had a teaching contract in Boston this fall, and Mike was based in California.

Reality was knowing that involvement with the dominant overwhelming, red-headed Pict had never been wise. They weren't alike. He was strong to her struggling. He was romantic and idealistic, whereas life had culled those values from her. He had tons of courage, but she floundered daily for mere ounces of that same ingredient. He was an Everest climber, a trouble lover, a challenge finder. She valued safety— no excuses and no exceptions.

What had he warned her? *Don't waste any time thinking you're safe, Irish. Not with me.*

She felt as safe as rotting timbers. *What have you done, Carra? Let Irish orchids and the Blarney stone and fairy raths go to your head?* It might have been easier if she had. It was the man who'd gone to her head, not the trappings. And Mike, she was terribly afraid, already meant more to her than a hundred Aarons ever had or could have. Mike was becoming more important to her than life.

"Now I know I'm good-looking, Carra, particularly when it's pitch dark, but you've got to stop looking at me like I'm a raw steak ready for the grill."

She saw his open eyes, shook her head ruefully and reached down to kiss his forehead. "I thought you were sleeping."

"You're the one who should be." No movement of hers had wakened him, but he'd instinctively felt that she was troubled. After making love the second time, she shouldn't have had the energy for worry, but he'd misjudged her before. Carra, regrettably, liked to think. Every time she thought, he had trouble.

He reached out an arm and hauled her close to him. With a lover's ability to see in the dark, his gaze swept possessively over her tangled hair and soft eyes, her kiss-stung mouth and long, white throat. She looked and was well-loved. She belonged to him as surely as his own heart did. "You're a dangerous woman," he murmured.

Again she shook her head. "You're the dangerous one. Nothing like that has ever happened to me before."

"Nor for me. Did you think otherwise?"

The tender whisper shook her. When he looked at her a certain way, when he touched her, she felt the pull of magic and the draw of something mystical. It wasn't that he could make her believe in things she didn't believe in, but when she was with him she wanted to.

"Are you sleepy?" he murmured.

She nodded, a fib without words. Absently she ran a fingertip along the line of his shoulder. His muscles bucked beneath her touch. She dipped her finger in the hollow of his throat and watched with fascination when his Adam's apple jumped.

"You're not acting at all sleepy, Irish."

"I am. I am." Desire never touched her mind, only awareness. He seemed to respond so powerfully to her. She'd never fathomed why. Mike seemed to have illusions that she was as strong as he was, as free and sure as a person. When she was with him, she wanted to be. When she was with him, she felt heady feelings about herself as a woman. She felt powerful and good and just a trace wicked.

None of that would be real in the morning, she knew, but it was dark now. Dark, and the rain was beating against the windows, and Mike was right there. His flat nipples hardened into stones when she touched them. He was ticklish. The lightest skim of her finger on the line of his hips, and good Lord, the devil rose.

Mike chuckled, claimed her hands and wound them behind her. The action made her breasts protrude; both needed a kiss. He kissed each, one at a time, with reverence and tenderness and gentleness. Then he lashed both breast tips with his tongue, heard her gasp of breath and immediately folded her, chin tucked high, under the quilt again. "We're going to give you one more opportunity to behave," he murmured teasingly.

"Didn't you know? The words *obedience* and *woman* haven't been linked in this decade."

He sighed, reclaimed her roaming hands and pulled them around his neck where he had more control over them. "What have I let loose?" he asked the ceiling.

"A damsel in distress?"

"The damsels in those fairy tales were never insatiable. And the specific damsel in question should be exhausted and conceivably might be a little tender. The gentleman is trying very hard not to take advantage."

"You like me to touch you," she informed him smugly.

"I love you to touch me," he corrected, and immediately paid for that small admission. Her kisses started as soft, questing, tentative explorations of his willpower, shy forays into testing her power as a woman. "Ah, honey..."

Watching her open up—for him, with him—made him feel sky-high as a lover and a man. Urgency suddenly scented the night; he folded her under him and let his mouth cover hers like a hot blanket on an icy night. He was aware his kisses were rougher than hers, aware his breath came harsh to her softer breathing, aware that this woman alone triggered the total loss of gravity in his universe.

He took her as high as he knew how to take her as a lover, or maybe she took him. It didn't much matter who did the taking. The grail of pleasure was a mutual quest, and the giving of it the right of each.

When it was over, he fell back, taking her with him. Marvels danced under his closed eyelids, marvels and magic and stars. He couldn't have been more exhausted. He couldn't have been more aware of the richness she brought to his life, the emptiness he'd felt until he'd found her. "I love you, Carra," he whispered.

"Oh, Mike, I love you, too." But the intensity of his words caused a thick, soft mist to coat her eyes, blurring her vision. It wasn't just what he said, but realizing so fast, so hard, that she had the capacity to hurt him.

"I want your children, love. A hundred of them. You know that, don't you?"

She stilled in his arms. He opened both eyes and saw the sheen in hers. "You don't have to say that," she said softly.

Fast, before she could turn away, he framed her face in his palms. "*Have* to? Honey, if I wanted a fast affair, I would have taken you up on your offer weeks ago. I want an O'Neill-Fitzgerald alliance—the dangerous kind, the unseverable kind, the kind that includes children and rings." At her silence, he tried humor. "Perhaps I could back down from a hundred. We could start bargaining at a dozen kids. I'm easy, Irish. You can probably argue me right down to the exact number you want. You're not going to tell me that you don't want children, because you've told me in a thousand ways that you love them."

"Yes."

"That's the word I was hoping to hear."

She shook her head fiercely. "No, Mike. Not so fast. Listen, please." Her breath caught at the look in his eyes. His tenor was lazy, but the tension in his body told her something else. She had no illusions about the man she loved. He bulldozed anything in his path when he wanted something. It was for his sake that she couldn't let that happen, not this time, not about anything this important.

She said quietly, "I want you to know that I didn't make love because of children and rings and promises. I didn't make love to tie you down to a commitment—and especially a commitment made in an emotional moment. Take the moment, Mike, and know I've given it to you free and from my heart. Any talk about futures will wait for another time.''

She was trying to tell him, in the only way she knew how, that she loved him as a strong, sure woman loves a man. She loved him not for what he could give her, but simply because loving him was right. She meant the words as a gift from a woman who'd once been haunted by doubts about her own judgment, to the man who'd helped her refind the courage in Carra O'Neill.

"That's what you want?" Mike said quietly.

"Yes."

He knew she was as exhausted as he was. He tucked her close, made a spoon of her back to his chest and covered her with the quilt to her throat. Beneath the quilt his arm cuddled under her breast, and his thigh snugged against hers. In such a way a man protected a woman from the dragons and shadows of the night and, incidentally, made sure she wasn't getting away.

Mike intended to be Carra's last lover, her only lover, although she didn't know that yet. Minutes passed. Gradually her breathing evened, and in time the iron tension gripping his nerves eased, but he closed his eyes feeling sick.

He'd waited a very long time to hear the word *love* from Carra. That she was unwilling to talk futures still hurt, although he told himself he shouldn't have been surprised.

She'd been through a great deal because of a careless, insensitive man. He already knew those scars ran deep and expected that she was still waiting for the world to jump on her again. She still didn't really believe anyone would be there for her when the chips were down.

Mike intended to be, and over a long trek of time he knew he could convince her that he wasn't made of the same cloth as the man who'd left her. The problem was that neither had much more time at Glencorrah.

The same thought ran through his mind that had been running there since he met her. A woman that good needed a knight. Now, before the chance to win her was completely gone.

Within the next two weeks the rental cranes and giant earth movers disappeared. The size of the work crew diminished as the castle neared completion. By mid-July there was only one scaffold left where the parapet at the very top of the south tower hadn't been finished.

That last scaffold was a level wooden platform with no braces nor rails to mar the view from the top. From two hundred feet in the air the view was magnificent. There were dark blue cliffs in the distance, greens coiling and ribboning around the twisting waters of the Shannon, brown bog lands and meadows of yellow gorse.

At lunchtime the platform itself boasted a white lace tablecloth, crystal via Irish Waterford and gleaming sterling—extraordinarily fancy trappings for a lunch of rough-cut sandwiches and soggy chips. Sitting cross-legged in worn jeans and a bright red sweater, Carra viewed her lunch host with an expression of mixed bemusement and helplessness.

She hadn't had a sane conversation with Mike since the night they'd made love. Heaven knew, she'd tried.

She'd come to Glencorrah trumpeting values of self-sufficiency and strength, intending to rebuild faith in herself alone. She'd been wrong. *Alone* wasn't a sacred word. Caring for Mike had taught her that self-sufficiency and self-reliance could naturally coexist with the right man. Faith in herself and forgiving herself for past mistakes was a mountain, but not such a huge mountain. Not when loving Mike said something about herself—who she was as a woman, what she was worth and what she valued.

She'd tried to tell Mike—honestly, carefully, tactfully—a dozen times over the past two weeks that she wasn't so terrified of climbing mountains any more.

It was really rather remarkable. She'd changed.

And he'd gone stark raving insane.

"Thirsty, honey?"

"A little, thanks." With her chin cupped in her palm, she watched Mike pour plain old cider into a Waterford tumbler that cost her week's salary. Two mornings ago she'd wakened up to find her entire bed piled with roses. "How's the design for my trebuchet going?"

"Nearly done. You can have a look after dinner."

"Great," she said cheerfully. Last Saturday she'd begged him to have a look at the keep kitchen. The kitchen had to be operable in Glencorrah's "living museum," but a test run baking session had revealed a flaw in the ventilation system. Gallagher and Sean had been flummoxed. Mike hadn't, but solutions had been postponed when he'd leaned her up against the stone kitchen wall and kissed her senseless.

"Your training session with the women go all right this morning?" He nudged a second sandwich into her hand.

"Terrific. Moira's a tremendous asset. I think she missed her calling as a teacher." Of all the people who had applied for the head of the tourist staff position, Moira had the qualifications that particularly appealed to Carra. She had a no-nonsense, easy way with people, she loved Glencorrah as much as Carra did, and she'd picked up responsibilities so quickly she was fast running Carra out of a job.

After their first morning working together, Carra had been so elated she'd tracked down Mike to share her delight. She'd found him in the stables. He'd been in a definite mood to share her delight—via a lethally disgraceful roll in the straw.

Strange treasures kept appearing on her doorstep. A shamrock in a glass globe. Earrings in a box with a dancing green ribbon. And two Irish Dresden candlesticks had miraculously shown up on her fireplace, while a scarf in all the shades of blue there were had appeared on her pillow.

And then there was this. These days Mike no longer seemed interested in talking up a woman with the courage to climb mountains with him. He was too busy serving lunch on a two-hundred-foot-high parapet overlooking the entire world.

He lifted a chip. She shook her head firmly, not so much because she didn't want it, but because she was a little afraid she'd throw it. Lately she'd been throwing a lot of things. Her basketball skills were improving. Her daily frustration level could be measured in how many wadded-up paper balls reached her waste-basket.

What am I going to do with you, Fitzgerald?

"Sure you're full?" he insisted.

"Stuffed!" She leaned back, replete and tried to divert herself with the unique view of the Irish sky. Whipped-cream clouds floated by for her pleasure. The tang of a river breeze put a crispness in the air. There always seemed to be a wind in Ireland. A wistful, yearning wind.

Mike stretched next to her, eyes closed for the last few moments of rest before the afternoon's work began. She took in the look of his shaggy, wild eyebrows, sun-kissed skin, his windblown mass of copper hair.

She looked, and then she blocked his sun as she shifted over him. His eyes shuttered open just as she dropped a kiss on his mouth.

As she had guessed, her intended light peck changed the moment their lips fused. His hands went up to her hair, bracing her for pressure even before it happened. He did it. Converted a simple kiss into something heady and urgent and fierce with need.

By the time his mouth lifted from hers, she was facing the sky. Her breath was coming hot and fast, and her pulse was scrambling. So was Mike's. His features were sculpted in harsh, intense lines. He had the look of a man who passionately wanted and passionately needed. The games were all done when he kissed her.

If it wasn't for the honesty of those kisses, Carra would be frantic with despair. The romantic side of Mike was endearing, exciting, sweet. All his whimsy and nonsense spoke to something Carra had never believed in . . . but maybe, in her heart, always wanted to. Still, why would a man woo a woman who was already won?

"Ahem?"

She startled like a bolt. Mike didn't. He raised his head, but never turned around for the sound of the voice. "Try a dive in the Shannon from the top of the north tower, McIllenney."

"Now, I'd do that. I really would, but you bit my head off this morning making sure I'd catch you for a quick five during the lunch hour."

"Damn, so I did," Mike said irritably.

Mike turned that brooding scowl on her, and for a moment she was afraid he'd forgotten their audience. He studied her flushed face and soft eyes with brooding intensity, intimate possessiveness and an indefinable emotion—something naked, something raw, something that told her about a man's special brand of vulnerability. A month ago she would have fast shied from the starved look of this hungry falcon on the hunt. Now she absorbed his hunger like reassurance and was damn well determined to believe in what she felt, saw, believed. To hell with what he didn't say.

In time, at his own good speed, he finally shifted around so he was half lying on his elbows, a great position to glare at the foreman.

Sean pushed back his hard hat, glanced at their fancy lunch trimmings with absolutely no surprise in his expression and shot Carra a look that said: I'd shoot him if I were you, lass, he's that far gone. The smile he leveled at Mike was careful. "Far as I'm concerned, we could wait until another time. You were the one that wanted to discuss the get-together for the crew."

"What get-together?" Carra quickly scooted to a sitting position.

Mike said absently, "The work will be all done but the shouting in another week. The boys deserve some fun. I kind of figured we'd throw a pretty big shindig, but time keeps zooming by, and I haven't gotten around to doing anything about organizing it."

"Don't look at me," Sean insisted.

"I wasn't looking at you." He looked at Carra instead. "I had in mind starting out with a twentieth-century pickup load of the best Irish brew, but for the rest, doing it up fourteenth century. I thought the boys would get a kick out of that. You know, roasted boar, jousts and battles, armor and costumes and banners and stuff."

"Sounds like great fun," Carra agreed, and was promptly greeted with dead silence. Zombie-dead silence. Mike produced one of his incorrigible grins out of nowhere. Sean tried out one of his rare, gentlemanly smiles. "No," she said flatly.

More silence and such sick, fake grins she could have throttled them both.

"No," she repeated. "I have a thousand things to do over the next few days. I don't have time to organize something like that. You haven't *left* time, and I wouldn't even know how to begin."

In full view of Sean, God and Ireland, Mike stole a kiss—mouth-to-mouth, an outrageous bribe.

When push came down to shove, Carra figured she could handle the organization of his fourteenth-century shindig. She'd really gained the confidence to handle a great deal from the time she met Micheal Dougel Fitzgerald.

Except Micheal Dougel Fitzgerald.

The tapestry was a hunting scene with falcons, woven with silk threads in ambers and golds and greens. Climbing down from the ladder, Carra put her hands on her hips and murmured, "What do you think? Is it even now?"

Mike didn't answer. She shot him a rueful glance. He'd been standing in the doorway for a good fifteen minutes, arms across his chest, watching her work. Dust streaked his forehead, and his boots were caked with it. He looked worn and tired, and he was missing his smile. His eyes still sent her messages across the room that had her pulse doing a slow tap dance.

"All right. You don't care if it's even. I'm not surprised. The boys were helping me until about two hours ago, until they even got fed up with watching me straighten my tapestries."

She stretched, chasing out the kinks from a long day and surveyed the solar with a mercilessly critical eye. The chamber was finally finished after two days of nonstop work.

The chandelier hanging from the ceiling was wood and outfitted with a dozen beeswax candles, which had been lit once to show they'd been used. Both tapestries were hung, each authentic to the period. The window seat under the arched window held a woman's crewel embroidery hoops, the bright silk threads on white linen half finished, as if someone had just put them down.

Late afternoon sunlight drifted down in yellow waves on the round wooden tub, four feet in diameter, that was the only claim Glencorrah had to a bathtub. Fourteenth-century people weren't too enthusiastic about baths, but when they indulged, they bathed communally. Soap sat on the wooden ledge of the tub, a blend of animal fat mixed with wood ash, as it should be.

The fireplace was a hooded affair and six-feet-wide huge. An iron grate held giant logs and an ash keeper. The lord and lady's bedchamber was short on furniture, but the bed was Carra's pride and joy.

The huge thing was six hundred years old and made a twentieth-century king-size look paltry. The headboard was old oak, taller than seven feet and carved intricately with boars and bears and falcons and fierce, wild, mystical creatures. Pillows didn't exist as they did now, but contemporary mores had nothing on fourteenth-century bedding. The fine Irish linens were soft, and the coverings were fur—huge, soft white pelts, so heavy they'd press a woman down into the feather mattress, so thick that a woman could get lost in them if she didn't have a man at her side. The draperies were pulled and roped now, but Glencorrah's lady, if she had any sense, could tug them completely around the bed and make an enclave of privacy for herself and her lord.

"I still need a trunk," Carra said irritably. The only thing wrong with the entire room was clothes. No closet or wardrobe belonged; people didn't have them in that time. But for now she still had a box in the corner, draped high with gowns and cloaks that needed a place to be put away. "I think I told you I've looked at three trunks. None of them were right, Mike. Two were sixteenth century, and one was the right period but so ordinary."

Mike had yet to move from the doorway, and Carra hadn't stopped moving. She carried the ladder into the hall, straightened both tapestries for the second time, then wandered to the stack of clothes, picking up one item at a time to hold it to the light.

"I showed you all the costumes the women were making, didn't I? Women's fashions are really the funniest. Not theirs, ours. We talk about a layered look as if it were something we just discovered. A medieval woman started with a shift, see..."

She held up a white linen chemise to show him. It was see-through delicate, crushably thin, virgin white. "Not too modest, hmm? And no underpants for most women, though if you ask me, I'll bet a lot of women caught a cold on their fannies. Anyway, over the shift she'd just keep putting things on to adjust to the weather. First a tunic—she'd tie that up with a metal belt at the waist called a girdle, then a cloak. The cloaks were hooded in back with a long point called a liripipe. Crazy maybe, but very elegant, and those cloaks were made of fur or silk and sometimes lined with more fur or more silk."

Dropping the white linen shift, she dragged at her hair, frantic that the room be right. The solar and Great Hall were the key rooms in the castle and were always going to earn a tourist's attention. "Mike, does it look right? What do you think? If you see anything that looks modern, out of place—if I've missed something—"

Suddenly aware of how silent he'd been, she turned. And saw something in his eyes that made her pulse start rattling. Mike had been very good for the past two days. Very good, she repeated in her mind for a third time.

"I think," Mike said slowly, "that if I were a marauding knight, intent on plunder and ravishment and claiming spoils, this is the first room I would come to. I think that I would take one look at that bed and forget all about conquering castles and battles. And I think that if I happened to find an Irish wench in that bed with raven-black hair and blue eyes, dressed in a white linen shift with her feet bare ... I think she wouldn't have that shift on for long."

He moved forward slowly, a step at a time. Carra found herself smiling and backing up a careful step at a time. "There are people around," she reminded him, her tone cheerful and wonderfully brisk.

"Not in the keep there aren't."

"Mike. It's the middle of the afternoon; I have tons to do."

"The conquering knight had rights of ownership, didn't he? The right to take any and all. He owned what he won in battle. Including the lady of the house."

"True, it was a disgusting, pagan time. No morals, no honor. I told you." The back of her knees bumped the bed edge. She took a sideway step. So did Mike. Her heart was thumping like a drum.

"I wonder what the lady of the castle felt like. To have a knight step into her room, sweat stained and battle weary, the taste of victory still in his mouth, the spirit of conquering still in his head. I wonder if she felt helpless, knowing he was going to take her. I wonder if she felt excitement.''

"She probably felt scared.''

"You think so?'' He cornered her at the wall by the headboard. He raised both her hands, layered them against the smooth stone wall and moved in, hips impaling her hips, body impaling her body. "I think she might have told herself she should feel scared,'' he whispered. "But my best guess is...she felt excitement.''

She saw his eyes, bright and hard, coming toward her, and then his mouth took hers. Illusions and fantasies rushed through her bloodstream. Knowing they were illusions didn't ease her trumpeting pulse.

He kissed with a victor's arrogance. His chin had a beard scratch, and she could smell sweat, the real sweat of a man who'd spent a day in physical work—or in a battle. Armor couldn't have been harder than his chest. He rocked his hips against her in a blatant statement of who was the stronger, the more physically powerful. And his tongue swept her mouth with plundering thoroughness, a ravishment of the senses that deliberately communicated what he wanted. What he was going to take.

She was no fourteenth-century lady. He was no marauding knight. It was just a game. Her head knew it was just a game, but her mouth didn't. Her mouth trembled under his, her heart fluttered like a trapped bird. Adrenaline pumped through her blood as if she were in real danger, and so, damn him, did excitement.

He never let her free long enough to take off clothes—just her jeans, and her underpants skidded off with them. Her bare fanny cuddled on soft white fur when he tossed her onto the bed, a move undoubtedly intended to look macho and dangerous. The man that covered her looked exactly that. Macho. Dangerous.

His tongue was as wild as his hands. He never gave her a chance to breathe, to think. He threw her legs up and high, and she told herself she couldn't possibly be ready, yet for that first plundering push her body closed around him like a hot, wet sheath.

Her fingers raked his back; her mouth returned, not soft kisses but bites, nips. She wanted him like earth, sun, air. She needed him like fire. Time spun back six hundred years. This knight had fought for her. This knight had won, because he was the strongest, the boldest, the bravest.

This knight could have anything he wanted and then some. "I love you. Love you," she cried.

The crest of pleasure that swept over both of them had nothing of rainbows or softness. It was an agony of pagan pleasure, real, harsh, sharp. And after they both burned themselves high and hot on that blaze of fire, they lay still. Panting, breathing-hard still. Exhausted, limp still.

Mike found the energy to shift to his side, only because he was terrified of crushing her. Carra, beneath him, had her eyes still closed. Soft little breaths were still puffing from her mouth; her forehead was damp, her mouth a dark rose from the pressure of his kisses.

She opened one eye and looked at him half in a daze. Her warrior Pict was gone. The devil looked exhausted, disheveled, disgustingly smug, and his incorrigible grin swept over her head to toe. "Well?"

Even his tone was sassy. "Well what, you devil?"

"Was she scared, Irish? Or did she feel... excitement?"

"You know exactly what she felt."

"I think... I hope... she felt a little of both."

Her heart abruptly stopped clanging and stilled. Mike's eyes no longer held the arrogance of a ravisher, the spirit of a conqueror. They were just a man's eyes, a rich, deep golden-green reflecting a man's fears and a man's anxiety.

She shook her head, raising up on an elbow. "She felt love," she whispered fiercely. "No fear, Mike. Just the excitement of wanting you. Of feeling safe with you. Of being taken by you because there's nothing else on earth she wanted more than to be taken by you. Tomorrow, today, yesterday. This way, any way you want."

What else could she tell him? How much plainer could she make it that she had courage now, courage and the strength to know what she wanted, strength and the love to offer him that he'd once asked for?

It was an ideal time for him to press for something, anything that would indicate he wanted a relationship with her beyond Glencorrah.

He didn't.

She'd been vulnerable to hurt before, but not like this. Trusting Mike had become part and parcel of re-learning to trust herself. All she could think of was that if she had made a mistake in judging Micheal Fitzgerald—the depth of his feelings for her, the future they had together, the needs and trust and wanting they shared—she knew she would lose a part of Carra O'Neill that she would never get back.

Nine

Ireland is never hot. Carra took a damp cloth to her cheeks and mentally repeated: Ireland is never hot.

"The boar's tender enough to make finger food, lass. If you've got some platters—"

"Right here." She handed Sean platters and utensils, noting that his face already had a whiskey flush. He wasn't the only one.

Mike's fourteenth-century shindig was in full swing, and the castle's inner courtyard was jammed with people. The construction crew made up big enough numbers on their own, but Carra had also invited every local she could call or coax into coming here, primarily because she had no intention of being the only woman.

Brogues thick as molasses rolled through the air, so did laughter. Many had made an obvious effort to come in costume. Men in leather jerkins and tights were sipping whiskey just as fast as men in jeans. Women in tunicked gowns and fancy headcaps were downing punch just as fast as the women in plaids and homespun wools.

Long trestle tables were loaded with breads and salads and delectable-looking pastries. Red Hugh's had been coaxed into going into the catering trade, but feeding three hundred was still no small task. It was a rotten task for a woman who'd had the absolute insanity to dress in costume on a ninety-degree day.

Carra's shift was cream linen with a puff at the bodice and sleeves. The sleeves showed through an ankle length tunic of a soft yellow wool. A gold girdle cinched in her waist, and her hair was covered with a cream wisp of a veil, waist long, held to her head by a braided cap. Wimples had been in style in the fourteenth-century.

She looked authentic.

She felt authentically hot.

"Do we have any more napkins?" Devlin asked her.

"No problem." As people milled toward the trestle tables, her hands moved as fast as her feet. Once the group was fed, games were scheduled—a javelin toss first, jousts last. Her eyes kept straying toward Mike, who was as busy as she was, if not more.

He was dressed in a sleeve-billowing pirate shirt and leather jerkin and was standing alone in the bed of the pickup-turned-bar. His hair was blowing like crazy, and his laughter was a roar of delight. He loved the crowd and was never surrounded by less than one, but more than once she caught his eyes darting across the throng of heads, searching for her.

Every time their eyes met, she felt despair shimmer through her. *We've only a few days left, Mike, and I'm so damned scared.*

Moira O'Brien moved next to her side when they were on cleanup detail. The big, rawboned woman stopped working long enough to give her a hug. "I'm going to miss you when you're gone, honey."

Carra smiled affectionately. "Nonsense. You can't wait to have me out of your sight and Glencorrah all to yourself. You've already got the tourist staff eating out of your hands. You're going to do fine."

Moira shook her head. "They're a good group, aren't they? But it was you that trained them; I wouldn't have known how to begin. When's the date you have to leave, lass?"

Carra wanted to answer and couldn't. At most, she could justify staying here another week. Moira had taken to the job like butter on bread, so Carra knew she was no longer necessary. And Mike really could have left the week before. She'd long guessed that his work contract with Mr. Killimer was unusual. An architect was rarely expected to oversee every last nut and bolt. Even granting Mr. Killimer's noninvolve-ment, Mike had taken responsibility for more than he should have to, and the nuts and bolts were long done.

Her gaze swept the perimeters of her castle, the curtained walls and towers, the parapets and high im-penetrable stone walls of the keep. She'd come here hoping the castle would guard her heart. She'd come here believing she wanted nothing more than to be as

invincible and strong as the stone foundation of
Glencorrah. She'd told the boys in training that a castle this strong could hold out as long as the will to resist remained.

That was still true for Glencorrah but not for her.
The man who'd laid siege to her heart had it. Her will
to resist no longer existed, and her pride in standing
alone had turned into her pride in loving a man. He'd
won his siege. The drawbridge was down, the castle
was undefended. And Carra was hurting like hell.

Moira was looking at her curiously, which was not
surprising considering that Carra had her mind on
fairy raths and shamrock salads and *meidhreach magairlín*—even though there were a thousand things to
do. She smiled quickly. "You're not really worried
about my leaving, are you? You can contact me if you
run into any problems."

"It won't be the same as having you here—but never
mind for now. I can see our conversation's about to be
interrupted."

"Pardon?" She turned to see Mike striding toward
her, a seven-foot-long spear in one hand and a long
yellow ribbon in his other, a crowd gathered behind
him.

She knew trouble when she saw it. He swooped
down on her like a warrior for prey, all red face and a
conquering grin. "There's been a challenge made for
this lady's honor!" He roared to the crowd. "Her fate
and her future will be in the hands of the conquering
knight. Should anyone care to witness a battle to the
death—a true fourteenth-century joust in which this
woman's virtue—" his voice ducked to a whisper

"—and her body and her mouth and her long, long legs, and her—"

"Micheal!"

He roared again, "I guess just her virtue is at stake, lads. First, though, the lass has to be talked into wearing my colors." Again his voice lowered just for Carra's ears. "Now where the devil do you wear these colors, Irish?"

"On the sleeve—what are you doing? The jousts were scheduled last," she reminded him.

"Change in schedule." He laced the yellow ribbon around her upper arm, and then kissed her fast, just a roguish slash of lips and a dominant male claiming. She tasted a bare trace of whiskey on his mouth and a hint of another taste—something desperate, something urgent. She had to be imagining it, because his voice was immediately like normal. "They're all revved up for the jousts now."

"But—"

"Trust me," he whispered. "Trust me, honey."

Maybe Mike had never given her any choice not to. Now, though, he clasped a hand through hers and pulled her along through the crush of bodies toward the bailey in front of the keep. The swarming partiers were high on whiskey, laughter and good food. They were game for anything, perhaps because Mike had invested a reckless spirit of fun in the day.

Silk banners had been hung with string and waved wildly under the hot, beating sun. A dais had been set up with a single chair in its center. Hands on her waist, Mike lifted her high and up and onto the platform, making her cheeks flush beet red. "It wasn't supposed to be me up here," she whispered frantically.

"Aren't you silly? It was always going to be you, Irish." And then he was gone.

It was a heck of a thing he'd done, stranding her alone on that platform, the center of attention when he knew darn well she hated being the center of attention. Jousting for a lady's honor was a scheduled part of the festivities, but Mike had promised her he'd choose from the local women.

He'd fibbed, but there was no doing anything about that now. At least the dais had an umbrella-type covering that blocked out the blistering sun, and the chance to sit was welcomed. Heck. The whole thing was meant in fun. The boys had worked darn hard for Glencorrah. Carra gradually caught the spirit of enthusiasm. This was no time to be a fuddy-duddy—or to let heartache show.

Several of the boys passed, patted her hand and mourned the threat to her virtue. She played out the role of a fourteenth-century lass in trouble; she got the group laughing and never looked up for some time. When she did, her smile faded like a sun behind clouds.

McIllenney was the challenging knight, as she could have guessed. Sean had the black horse, Mike the white. Where they'd found such beautiful horses she had no idea, but marvelous horseflesh wasn't hard to find in Ireland. The nags wore each knight's ribbon and gold bridles and had their tails all fancily braided. All of that was in keeping with joust etiquette; so were the seven-foot spears and the wearing of armor.

But it was the wearing of armor that had her smile gone. This wasn't the fourteenth century, and there were times one compromised when needs must. Needs must. It was ninety degrees in the blinding sun; the baked courtyard added to the heat, and both men had had a bit of whiskey. Sean showed some sense. He was putting on the basic breastplate vest and ignoring the headgear.

Mike wasn't showing any sense at all. The crowd of men gathered around him were egging him on, fitting him into an entire armor suit. A frown dug into her brow. When she saw him tug on the metal helmet, she was standing. Dammit, he was crazy. He'd bake in the metal, and the whole suit weighed close to a hundred pounds. "Mike!"

An enclave of people had gathered around her ostensibly to keep the lady from fleeing her fate. It was part of the game. She tried to tell herself he'd be fine. It would be over in seconds.

The games weren't over in seconds, though. Both knights started off by parading their horses around the bailey with a flourish and pageantry that the crowd loved. Rolls of laughter and approval filled the air, and then Gallagher shot an arrow in the air, the signal that the joust would begin.

The rules were simple. The first man who either cried uncle or was pushed off his horse was the loser. It was hardly a battle to the death, and the spear edges were blunted, set up for show, not to hurt anyone. Yet all sound died when the black and white knights poised at their starting lines, lances facing each other, competition as real in the air as if the battle were real.

Men, Carra thought fleetingly, and tried to smile when someone patted her arm. The horses went thundering toward each other; she heard the clash of metal. Yells streaked the crowd, then total silence when the knights faced each other again. That first clanging encounter told Carra that Mike and Sean must have prearranged how they'd handle the battle—how to make it look real without either of them risking getting hurt.

The joust was no danger. The danger was heat. Her fingers tightened on her arms, feeling oddly chilled. Sun glinted off the metal on Mike's head like a mirror of silver. The knights crashed toward each other again. And again. And a fourth time. The crowd got wilder every time; they wanted more.

She was standing for the fifth clash. She could see Sean's wet forehead gleaming in the sun, saw him wipe his hand across his face, knew how hot he was. Take off the headplate, Mike. Take off at least the damned headplate and do it now.

"I'd like to get your personal impressions of all this, Miss O'Neill." A stone-faced reporter with a wet brow was trying to pluck her sleeve. Hours before she'd been delighted the press had shown up for their party—it couldn't be better publicity for the opening of Glencorrah.

"Not now. Please!" The sixth clash and she saw Mike stagger, nearly lose his balance on the horse.

"I'll have your lady, Fitzgerald!" Sean yelled.

"Never!"

The sound of Mike's voice drained the last of color from her face. His tenor was never less than clear and sharp. The crowd assumed his stagger was more show. What terrified her was that Sean could also assume his stagger was show, especially since the white knight had thirty pounds on him and a good six inches in height.

"Stop it!" She yelled, but no one heard her—or no one was listening. The knights faced off for the seventh confrontation. Carra jerked the wimple off her head, lifted her skirts halfway to kingdom come and jumped off the platform. All she could think of was speed, and all the crowd could think of was competition.

She heard a sudden wave of sound through the people—a sound that stopped her heart and sent fear climbing clear to her throat like something thick and unyielding and unbearably hot. She couldn't get through the mass of bodies. "Tell them to stop it! It's over. Tell them it's over." It wasn't that people didn't hear her but they didn't really comprehend. They thought it was part of the game, part of the roles and rules from another time.

She heard the clash of metal again, the silence when she knew the knights were again facing off. The crush of bodies was claustrophobic; she smelled sweat and whiskey and felt sick. She made it through, finally; she made it through in time to hear a huge roar, a white and a black horse bearing down on each other in a fury, spears raised....

The wind stopped; the sun stopped; the people disappeared. Glencorrah faded somewhere mystical, somewhere soft. All she saw was the armored giant falling in slow motion, Sean bearing down on him with the raised spear, prancing hooves, laughter terrifyingly loud. No one knew but her. No one but her seemed to realize what was happening. Damn them, damn them...

She ran, but Mike had already crashed to the ground. Sean leapt from his horse and came running as fast as she did, but she reached him first. She knelt in the dust, pushing frantically at the hot heavy helmet.

"Mother Macrae, lass, I don't understand. I never touched him. The whole world knows he's a ton stronger than me; it was all just in fun—"

"It's heat," she blazed at Sean, and for just a few seconds made eye contact. He understood. "Get water, cloth, the people away from here."

It was all she could do to manage the heavy armor, but heaven knew no one was more qualified than she was to know exactly how it came on and off. And she knew exactly how much trouble Mike was in when she finally pulled off the headpiece and saw his face, clammy and leeched of color, his eyes unable to focus.

The armored leggings wrapped at the thighs. She stripped at them, clawed at them. For the breastplate she had to shift him on his side, and her giant was so huge, so heavy. "Damn you, Mike, damn you, Mike, I'm going to shoot you when this is over; I'm going to tie you up in a child's crib where you belong; I'm going to..." She loosened the leather ties at his back, arms aching, fingers fumbling, and when she was finally able to drag off the top armor, nearly crumbled at the weight it took to pull it off him.

"Carra, for God's sake, lass, let me help you."

Sean probably could, if she would just let him physically closer to Mike. Unfortunately, there was no chance she could face leaving his side.

Fast, there was a soaked cloth in her hand, thankfully not icy but lukewarm. Too cold could produce shock, but she had to get his body temperature down and fast. "We need a doctor, and we need to get him out of the sun." She dribbled water in his mouth, cooled his cheeks and forehead, ripped at his shirt so she could get to his chest. "Get his shoes off, the socks. Mike, open your eyes. Open your eyes, dammit, please?" To Sean she said fiercely, "I'm going to kill him. I just want you to know that. When this is over, if he's not all right, if he's not perfectly all right I'm going to kill him."

When Mike opened his eyes, it was to a disorienting sense of blurred vision and vague dizziness. It was pitch dark, and he seemed to be lying in Carra's bedroom, buck naked under a single sheet. The clock on her bureau read ten minutes after one.

He had a memory of being carried, a memory of being immersed in water, a memory of a doctor's brogue so musically colorful that he never understood a word, a memory of darkness. He also had a memory of Carra. Her face had been blanched white, and her eyes had been a sapphire fire of anxiety, his yellow banner streaming from her arm.

The banner was gone. Carra wasn't. Her face was still stark white, and she was leaning over him the minute he was able to focus. "Water, Mike," she whispered softly. "It'll taste good and feel good. Just a little."

But it wasn't water she gave him but a chip of ice. It melted on his tongue, slid past a throat that still felt dry and tight. His stomach...had been better. So had his pride.

"Everyone had a good time. You give great parties, Irish." His voice sounded a little cracked and a little strange, but it was functional.

"Shut up, Mike. I'm so mad at you I can hardly talk." But the soft rag she soothed on his forehead was gentle, cooling, soothing. She was still in costume, though the yellow gown looked dirt stained and wrinkled. She also had it hooked up halfway to her waist in order to kneel on the bed. She reached over his bare chest, sliding the cool cloth down his arms and shoulders. "You missed a fine argument between me and the doctor. Stupid man! He says you'll be fine in twenty-four hours if we keep fluids going and have you rest for a day. What kind of advice is that? I told him you were staying in bed for a week. Heat prostration is no joke." She stopped her gentle washing only long enough to wag a finger at him. "You're not moving except to the bathroom. Meals in bed and no work, and you don't even walk without my say-so. I repeat, no work, Fitzgerald. Give me an argument and see what happens."

"When," he murmured, "did you get so bossy?"

"How could you do that to me? You scared me half out of my mind! You have more sense, I know you do. You must have realized how heavy and hot that armor was, how broiling it would be under that sun."

"I thought—"

"You thought what?"

He looked at her, all that fury, all that rage. Carra would have him believe she was halfway to slugging him. The tears flooding her eyes told him something else. "I wanted to be a knight for you, Irish. I still do."

"A knight!" Frustrated beyond belief, she wadded up the cloth and threw it clear to the far wall. "I must have told you a thousand times that I'm a realist, not a romantic. Darnit, Mike, I never wanted some crazy image of a knight. All I wanted was a man. I wanted you."

He patted the sheet next to him. "I'll explain. If you'll slip out of those clothes."

"No!"

"All of them. And climb into bed with me."

"Mike, this is no time for nonsense. You're weak as a cat. I want to be up and taking care of you. You need as much liquid as you can take in, and—"

"And I intend to be sleeping at two o'clock in the morning, not drinking, honey. You're going to be sleeping, too. Now I'm fine . . . or I will be once you cuddle in here. Please?"

She'd noticed before that his low-pitched tenor had magical powers. Other times that tenor had unraveled a woman's mind, destroyed a woman's sound common sense. It seemed it did so again.

Truthfully she was so tired that she barely had the strength to tug off the yellow tunic, the pale linen shift. The doctor had left four hours ago, but Gallagher and Sean had stayed until a half hour before. There had been nothing anyone could do for Mike by then but watch him rest and make sure he had liquids when he wanted them. One o'clock in the morning and her body craved release from the punishment of stress and tension she'd put it through.

Bare finally, she slipped in next to him, not touching—except to coax another ice chip onto his tongue. He still looked pale-gray, and for Mike to be lying absolutely still was so unlike him that it tore at her heart. At least his eyes looked normal again, clear and bright, and, she noted dryly, fully cognizant of her state of undress.

He may not have much immediate strength but enough to reach out an arm and drag her closer. Close enough so he could turn his head and drop a kiss on her forehead, close enough that he could feel the exhaustion start to yield inside her from the touch of flesh to flesh, the comfort of skin to skin.

"I like you naked, Carra."

She draped an arm across his chest, not, he knew, in desire, but because the wench wanted to check his heartbeat. He captured her hand and dragged it around his neck where it belonged.

"I'm not going to stay here if you don't immediately go to sleep," she warned him.

"Yes, you are. You're going to be here a long, long time, honey, so you might as well get used to it." He closed his eyes, absorbing the feel of her soft, supple skin, the touch of her lips in the hollow of his shoulder. "You said you wanted me, Carra, but you've had me from the day I met you. From that very first day you also made clear what you didn't believe in. Romance. You had images of champagne and moonlight linked inevitably to the kind of man who wouldn't be there when the chips were down.''

"Mike—"

"Shh." He kissed her forehead, her nose. "That's exactly why I wanted to be a knight for you, Irish. I wanted to be the man to put the dance of magic and laughter back in your eyes. I wanted you to know that the romance and reality of loving don't have to be at war. Maybe true knights rarely existed in history. Maybe the code of chivalry was not so romantic, but some things have always been true, Carra. I'm talking about honor and loving and the way things should have been, the way things always should be, between a man and a woman no matter what period of time they live in."

"Mike . . ." Her voice was helpless. She thought of a man who'd pushed her into that horrible little bar to handle being on her own in a group of men, a man who'd coaxed her into confronting McIllenney alone, a man who'd teased and pushed her into tackling the giant responsibilities of Glencorrah when she'd been so terribly afraid she couldn't handle them.

Knights twentieth-century style were a little different than the old breed. Knights twentieth-century style encouraged a woman to be strong, not weak. Encouraged a woman to believe in herself instead of depending on other people. Encouraged a woman to take the giant, huge, overwhelming risk of loving when the courage wasn't there and life had warned her not to and she had no promises and no guarantees. Except she did have the faith that the man was good and that loving was right.

"You are a knight to me," she said softly. She peppered soft kisses on his face—all light, all careful, all tender. "You have been all along, Mike. I've tried to tell you how much I loved you."

"The lady had been hurt. The way I saw it, the lady needed time. And wooing. And as many doses of *meidhreach magairlín* as I could give her, because there's a love born of need and a love born of magic, and the two together work best. It's magic I wanted you to believe in, honey. A magic that'll last us until our rocking-chair days, a magic strong enough to last through time." He opened his eyes, lifting the strands of hair away from her face. He said quietly, "Marry me, Carra."

"Yes."

"Louder."

"*Yes*. For the magic. For the reality. Both are real, Mike. At least they are for me. God, I love you."

Smiles passed from one to the other, so soft, so secret, so private that the moon shone bright as sunlight and the shamrock fields outside the cottage gleamed silver. No one else, of course, would have seen the silver fields, the sunlight-bright moon. This was a magic reserved for two, a magic as lustrous and real as the softness in Carra's eyes. Mike couldn't stop looking at her and didn't try.

"The little people offered me a vision last night, Irish."

"Did they?"

He noticed a definite lack of skepticism in her voice. He chuckled, a sound low and rumbling from the very back of his throat. "This vision," he continued gravely, "was of a lass coming down the stairs from the solar in a wedding dress. I saw a chaplain in the Great Hall, waiting with an open prayer book. I saw knights and pages and waiting women, and I heard trumpets. I saw banners waving."

"A wedding at Glencorrah?"

"And one of the few things Mr. Killimer and I haven't argued about. We have his full approval, and the only question is timing. I have in mind a private ceremony, which definitely means before the castle's open to the public. In fact, I have in mind tomorrow—"

"Tomorrow!" The loving mist lifted from her eyes long enough to give him a chiding frown. "You crazy man. Someone let you out too long in the sun— namely me. See if I ever let you out of my sight again."

"Carra?"

"Hmm?"

"I had another thought."

"No, you don't. You are not strong enough."

"I could try."

"No, you can't."

She was wrong, although their loving was less fireworks than tenderness. Less a shout and a roar of passion than whispers of deep-felt love and lasting trust.

They slept, but both wakened in the wee hours of the morning. Mike wanted to talk about moving his work base to Boston. Carra insisted it would be easier for her to find another teaching position in California. They saved the rest of that discussion for the days to come, since neither doubted they would easily find a workable compromise. It seemed more important to name their children.

They named more children than the two of them could possibly have in a hundred years, which was perfectly logical to Carra. In a romantic, magical sense their love had already lasted six hundred years.

One man's dream of Glencorrah had taken six hundred years to become real.

Carra figured that was nothing compared to how long she expected to love Micheal Dougel Fitzgerald, and he seemed to be of a similar mind.

*   *   *   *   *